THE KAT
AND THE
HOOLIGOATS

and Suet Begins

BARRY HUDLEY

Matador
9 Priory Business Park,
Wistow Road, Kibworth Beauchamp,
Leicestershire. LE8 0RX
Tel: 0116 279 2299
Email: books@troubador.co.uk
Web: www.troubador.co.uk/matador
Twitter: @matadorbooks

ISBN 978 1800463 707

British Library Cataloguing in Publication Data.
A catalogue record for this book is available from the British Library.

Printed and bound in Great Britain by 4edge Limited
Typeset in 12pt Minion Pro by Troubador Publishing Ltd, Leicester, UK

Matador is an imprint of Troubador Publishing Ltd

Dedicated to;

TRUFFLE

Also to THE HOOLIGOATS, who related this story to me and, hoof-on-heart, have assured me that it is, mostly, true.

My thanks to;

JO, SAM and KATY for inspiring me to write, with special thanks to KATY, for her expert advice, guidance, and encouragement in bringing this book to fruition.

And to JANE, for reading lots of drafts from an adult's point of view, and always laughing at the right points.

Also, of course, to the team at MATADOR, and illustrator DAVE HILL, who have made Elf-Publishing such a pleasure.

—

THE HOOLIGOATS want to thank TARA and the team, plus all of the children at YORK HOUSE SCHOOL in Rickmansworth, where the goats have become key members of a group of animals dedicated to the emotional welfare of the schoolchildren.

Profits from the sale of this book will go to BUTTERCUPS SANCTUARY FOR GOATS in Kent, the UK charity that specialise in the welfare and care of goats that have been neglected, ill-treated or abandoned. (buttercups.org.uk)

Chapter One

The Present

—

I know it's my twelfth birthday, and I'm sure I'll be okay soon, but I'd prefer it if no-one says 'Happy Birthday, Ginger Kat!'. Not today. This isn't a morning for celebration, and I don't think there's anything that can change that.

Not like that Sunday just a few weeks ago, which is when my *other* life actually began. In many ways, it was the weirdest and most wonderful day of my life, even though it led up to what happened yesterday. And, yes, maybe I should have spotted the warning signs earlier. But I was naive then. Not so much, now. Especially because, in spite of everything, I still can't get Hooligoat Ralph's 'pigs-might-fly' project out of my head.

The Sunday in question began pretty much like any other, apart from the fact that school holidays had just begun. Marcas, my best friend, had stayed overnight in our spare room, and joined Mom, Pop and I as we sat down for breakfast together. Although we don't do the full vegan thing, we all love animals, so Sunday breakfast tends to be more pastries and cheeses rather than bacon and sausages and stuff.

Pop was as jovial as ever. Just a few minutes into our meal, he peered over his spectacles and looked inquisitively at Marcas and I.

'So,' he said, 'did you two spot any more ghosts while you were exploring the ruins at the Priory yesterday?'

Indelicate, I know, but I had a mouthful of croissant, so Marcas shook his head and answered, 'No, Mr Briscoe, nothing yesterday.'

I swallowed my food, almost choking in the process. 'But,' I added, 'it's been almost a year since we saw the ghost of a monk pointing at us in the Chapter House so I'm sure we'll get to see another one soon. Maybe even one of the nuns this time.'

Pop tilted his head slightly to one side. 'Mmmm, are you quite sure that *was* a ghost, Kat? It might just have been your imagination, or somebody dressed up in a monk's frock.'

'Firstly, Pop,' I said, taking a sip of water, 'Marcas and I both saw the figure floating along in the air about five metres above us and, secondly, monks didn't wear frocks, they wore habits. It was a ghost. Everyone knows that Wenlock Priory is haunted, and if we were allowed to stay there overnight we'd be able to do some real ghost-hunting.'

Pop nodded gently, as usual ignoring my point about going ghost-hunting, and turned to Mom. 'What do you think, Sarah? Do you reckon it was a ghost?' He smiled innocently. 'Or was it just a bad habit?'

Marcas chuckled, until I playfully kicked his shin under the table.

'Reginald, dearest,' Mom sighed, 'we have a conversation about ghosts every time we go to Much Wenlock and visit the Priory. The only thing I reckon is that I'm going to make some toast.' She stood up and went into the kitchen.

'Well I never,' said Pop, giggling quietly to himself. 'Toast for a ghost. Let's hope they like sourdough.'

–

Breakfast was a very relaxed affair and we must have sat there for about an hour, but at the end of it Pop suddenly sprang into action like a puppet on strings.

'I think,' he said dramatically, standing up and flinging his arms wide as though he was addressing a big audience, 'it's time for our Sunday Morning Yomp.'

The Yomp took place every Sunday after breakfast, no matter what the weather was like. And I know that *yomping* is something that soldiers do when they're marching over hills and things but, to be fair to Pop, the roads in our village do have a lot of potholes. Of course, although our yomps would usually be an excuse for Pop to have a gossip with the other villagers, the really great thing was that we'd always end up visiting The Hooligoats, four pygmy goats named Barney, Ralph, Fernando and Cuthbert. They lived at Pets Corner, a ramshackle place just on the edge of our village that used to be a dairy farm many years ago. It still had a big farmhouse, lived in by the rather crabby and reclusive Barbara Bradbury, and it even had a small café. Most of the barns had been converted into either aviaries for different kinds of birds, or stalls for animals to go in at night. There were a few Shropshire sheep, a couple of Kunekune pigs, a family of meerkats plus, of course, the four pygmy goats who became known as 'The Hooligoats'. The Hooligoats were, or rather *are*, four of the most loveable animals in the whole world, even though they are easily the worst behaved. I can also tell you that Pets Corner was the place that Marcas and I first met, so it'll always be a special place for us, despite everything that's happened. We often went there to visit The Hooligoats after school and at weekends, and whenever we were with them, I would wonder what tales they'd be able to tell us if only they could talk.

Anyhoo, after Pop's rather theatrical gesture, he went off to the hallway and came back with a bundle of coats, which he dropped onto his chair. With a flourish he added The Blue Bobble to the top of the pile.

He grinned at me. 'And here's the hat that Kat's Aunt Elsie bought for her.'

'No way,' I laughed. 'She didn't buy it, she knitted it. And it started off as a winter coat for her lop-eared rabbit, but she forgot to leave any holes for its ears to poke through. I know I told her that I'd love to wear a hat, but that's more like a tea-cosy with flowers painted on it. And that colour doesn't match my hair at all. Whatever could Aunt Elsie have been thinking?'

Pop chuckled, came over to me, and tousled my hair. 'Tell you what, Carrot Top,' he said, 'I'll save up my pocket money and buy you a lovely hat for your birthday. Either that, or we can wait for Santa to bring you one at Christmas?'

'Well,' I replied, 'I'm sure Santa would bring one that was a good colour match, but Christmas is too far away and I really would like a hat quite soon, so yes, a birthday one would be lovely, thank you.'

'Birthday it is.' Pop swayed from side to side, making a strange 'oohing' sound, presumably pretending to be a ghost. 'But now it's time...' he slowly flailed his arms around like an out-of-control windmill, '... time to go see what's happening in the Big Wide World known as The Village.'

Our village only has ten houses, plus Pets Corner, so it's actually really small, despite Pop's insistence on calling it the "Big Wide World". I couldn't resist one of our favourite bits of banter.

'So many jokes in one morning,' I teased him. 'You think you're funny, don't you Pop?'

'I used to,' he sighed, 'before you came along.'

—

Pop led the way out through the front door, pausing to breathe deeply to "take in the fresh country air". Then he noticed that Mr Brown, our next-door neighbour, was out weeding his front garden, so he strode off for a chat with him.

As Marcas and I hung back on the driveway to wait for Mom, Marcas leaned over and whispered to me.

'Were you joking just then? About Father Christmas, I mean?'

'No,' I replied. 'Why would you think I was joking?'

'Well, you do realise that no-one else in our class believes that Santa actually exists?'

'So? I happen to be different. I know it might sound crazy to others but, in a way, it's like the ghost we saw at the Priory. I have this feeling that there's… kind of… another world out there that we don't properly know about, don't understand. And Santa Claus is part of that world.'

'Oh, okay.'

'And what about you? Are you telling me that you don't believe?'

Marcas looked blankly at me, and raised his eyebrows. He didn't need to say anything.

I shrugged. 'Don't worry,' I said, 'we don't have to agree on everything.'

He turned his gaze towards Pop and Mr Brown. 'On a different subject,' he said, quietly, 'I know you're really proud of the colour of your hair, but don't you mind being called "Carrot Top"?'

'Not really, Carrot Top is fine from Pop, though I wouldn't want just anyone saying it.' I prodded him gently on his arm. 'And I certainly wouldn't want anyone using my birth-name either.'

'Ouch, and don't I know it,' Marcas said, playfully rubbing the top of his arm. 'I still have the bruises from when I called you Katherine last week.'

'You're such a drama-queen,' I said, prodding him again. 'But yes, you can call me Kat or The Kat, or even

Ginger Kat, but not Katherine. Anyway,' I shook out my curls, 'I like to think my hair is different, just like me. *And* it's my natural colour, unlike Mom's dyed blonde hair with strawberry-pink highlights and added curls.'

'Talking of your mother, wasn't she supposed to be coming with us?'

Sighing, I muttered, 'I'll go and see where she's got to this time.'

I turned and popped back into the house, only to find Mom still doing her window-checking thing. This had become something of an obsession of hers, and she was beginning to worry me. Not only would she check each of the windows to make sure they were closed and locked, but she'd also check the connecting door between the kitchen and the garage, even when the garage up-and-over door was locked. Some weeks prior, she'd even got Pop to shape a wooden board which she now used to block off the chimney. All very strange behaviour, I thought, even for an adult.

After hurrying Mom along, we eventually emerged through the front door.

Pop looked over at us and called, 'Come on you lot, or it'll be Monday before we get to see The Hooligoats.'

I turned to Marcas and said extra-loudly, 'Pop always does more talking than walking.'

As we marched off from the house, Pop told us what Mr Brown had been saying.

'Bad news, I'm afraid,' he said. 'Sounds like Mrs Bradbury wants to get rid of The Hooligoats. Seems she's going to use the space for a farming museum. Lots of old machinery, ploughs, that kind of thing. Sounds horrible, I know, but Mr Brown says the old lady isn't at all bothered about what happens to the goats, and if no-one adopts them they'll end up on her dinner plate.'

With that awful bit of news racing round our heads, Marcas and I walked several paces behind Mom and Pop, trying to work out how to persuade them that *they* should offer to house the goats. After all, we had plenty of room in the garden, and Marcas and I were used to helping Mr Gohturd, who looked after The Hooligoats, to muck out and put fresh bedding down for them. We'd probably need to put new fencing up, but that couldn't be too difficult, not for Pop. What I couldn't understand, of course, was how Mrs Bradbury could bear to get rid of them at all, even if they were so very naughty.

When we reached Pets Corner, we started to walk round the first enclosures, which was where the bird cages were. At this point Pop, rather stupidly I thought, put his face right up against the parrots' cage, something he'd often warned me not to do.

'Who's a pretty boy then?' he squawked at the birds.

'Not me, dingbat!' shrieked one of them, and it dived straight at Pop's nose. Pop just about managed to pull his face away before a sharp beak stabbed viciously through the mesh. At this, all of the other parrots began to shriek like klaxons, as though sounding an alarm. There was a stern voice behind us.

'Mr Briscoe, I do hope you're not annoying my birds. They're very sensitive, you know.'

We spun round to find Mrs Bradbury standing there, pointing a pitchfork menacingly in our direction.

'No, no, not at all,' replied Pop, carefully checking his nose for blood. 'In fact it was the other way round. I was being very friendly towards them and they attacked me. I should have known better – I've seen them peck at other visitors.'

'Huh. Don't get me started on "visitors",' retorted Mrs Bradbury haughtily. 'They must think I run this place for their benefit. One such "visitor" complained last week that Lord Fittlebasket, my prize Shropshire, had bitten her child-person's ear. Serves it right is all I can say, one should never try to hug a Shropshire just before feeding time.' She peered intently at Pop's nose before continuing. 'Hmmm. And I suppose these,' she looked with distaste at Marcas and I, 'are your children? I've seen the two of you here before, haven't I?'

For some reason, Marcas started to giggle.

'Marcas is just a friend,' I said, gently nudging him. 'He lives in the next village along. We both come to see The Hooligoats as often as we can.'

'Hooligoats?' said Mrs Bradbury. 'Hooligoats? Don't get me started on those horrid pygmy goats. Beastly little creatures they are. Some of our "visitors" seem to like them, but I think those goats are only good for one thing, and that's the stewing pot. And if no-one offers to have them by the end of next month, that's exactly where they'll end up. I've even gone to the considerable expense of buying another freezer, ready to store them in when they've been cooked.'

How could she be so awful? I felt myself getting cross and imagining that I was lunging at Mrs Bradbury and grabbing her by the throat, giving her a piece of my mind about eating poor defenceless little animals. I don't know if Pop could sense what I was thinking, but he put his hand on my shoulder as though he were trying to restrain me. Mrs Bradbury looked down her nose at me.

'I'm surprised you two child-persons haven't got your noses stuck in mobile phones. Isn't that what you all do these days?'

I shook my head, keeping as calm as I could, and replied politely, 'Actually, Mrs Bradbury, it's true that some of our friends have mobile phones and yes, a few of those do seem to be a little preoccupied with them, but Marcas and I worry about the rare minerals that are used in making phones, and about whether some of them are made using cheap labour. I mean, does that sound fair to you?'

Mrs Bradbury looked suspiciously at me. 'Er, well...' she muttered.

Before she could say any more, however, a blast of icy cold wind suddenly scythed its way through Pets Corner. It only lasted a minute, but we could see our breath forming little clouds of vapour in front of us, and we all started shivering.

'Wow,' cried Pop, as he pulled his collar up. 'What was that all about? Has Mary Poppins arrived?'

Mrs Bradbury was obviously not amused. 'What has the weather got to do with a fictional homehelp, may I ask?'

'Well,' Pop tried to explain, 'Mary Poppins floated in by umbrella when the wind changed direction. And that wind just came in from the nor—'

Mrs Bradbury held her hand up to silence Pop. 'Whatever that Poppins woman did, or did not do, is irrelevant. The only person that's arriving today is my niece, Ailsa, from Scotland, and I would imagine she'll arrive by taxi, not on some trifling little puff of wind.' She glanced at me, and with a final 'Huh, cheap labour indeed', stomped off, pitchfork still in attack position.

'Well,' I said when I thought she was out of earshot, 'you can understand why she's called Bossy Barbara.'

Pop laughed and loped off, doing one of his silly walks. I so wished BB would have turned round and spotted him.

As Mom and Marcas wandered after Pop, my skin suddenly tingled, and I had the strangest feeling we were being watched. It was such an intense sensation that even my goose-bumps developed goose-bumps. I looked around, but there was nothing unusual to be seen. Not unless you counted that parrot, though I suspected he was more bored than truly evil. I called out to the others, and ran to catch them up.

—

When we got to The Hooligoats' enclosure there were no goats to be seen, but I knew they couldn't resist linseed chips, so I got a fifty-pence piece from Pop and put it into the gumball machine that was on the wooden fence. A portion of small brown chips dropped down the chute.

I shared them with Marcas, and we each placed a few treats onto the open palms of our hands, so as not to get fingers nibbled, and leaned over the fence.

'C'mon lads, come and get some treats,' we shouted.

Sure enough, there was a commotion inside the shed and Barney appeared in the doorway, busily chewing some hay. He saw our outstretched hands and eagerly trotted out, closely followed by the other three Hooligoats. As usual, Barney was joined by Cuthbert and Fernando as they paced up and down along the fence, pushing each other around to try to get the best spot for being fed. Ralph, in the meantime, jumped up onto a wooden platform to keep out of reach of Barney's horns, which are much bigger than any of the others.

There was lots more jostling as each of them hungrily snuffled chips from one hand and then tried to move on to see if there were more treats in someone else's hand and, of course, we made sure to throw plenty onto the platform for Ralph. We must have bought seven or eight lots from the gumball machine, but The Hooligoats were worth it, especially as Pop was paying.

–

We stayed with The Hooligoats for at least an hour before Mom said it was time to get back for lunch. Marcas decided he needed to go home as well, so we said our goodbyes and he set off up the lane in the opposite direction to us.

I thought the walk back would be a good opportunity to test Mom and Pop out on the notion of us housing the goats in our garden, but Pop had already guessed what I was going to ask.

'Kat,' he said as he put his arm around my shoulders, 'I know you think we have a big garden, but we don't have anywhere near enough space for them, especially as we'd have to build a big shed to house them at night. Best thing we can do is ask around, try to find somewhere for them, maybe even someone with a small field that's not being used. If Mrs Bradbury keeps to what she says, we've got nearly two months to find something. So, cheer up, there's time to save them yet.'

I knew Pop was right, I just didn't want to admit it. The thought that the lads may end up as frozen curry made my stomach churn.

As we walked back towards home, I couldn't help thinking about The Hooligoats. It seemed so strange that Bossy Barbara would have gone to the trouble of buying the goats only two years earlier, and now wanted to get rid of them. Whatever could have happened to make her change her mind about them? More to the point, what would become of the lads? I racked my brain, trying to think of somewhere, anywhere, they would be safe.

As I pondered, my thoughts drifted back to the first time Marcas and I had seen The Hooligoats. Of course, they didn't have the nickname then, they were only a few months old when they first came to Pets Corner. They were such fluffy and cuddly little kids, and when we first got some linseed chips and went into their paddock, we sat down on the grass and let the goats climb all over us.

That was such a wonderful day, and we must have spent ages with them, playing and feeding treats to them.

–

Anyhoo, when we reached home, Mom unlocked the front door and went inside, followed by Pop and then me. After taking her jacket off she hurried in, went straight to the living room and sat down, while Pop went into the kitchen to make some more coffee.

Mom looked at me, a huge smile on her face. 'One o'clock, and all is well,' she said, contentedly.

At that point, Pop came through from the kitchen. When she saw what he was carrying, Mom went pale and froze.

'Odd,' said Pop, as he shrugged his shoulders. 'I could have sworn this wasn't on the kitchen table when we went out.' He held out a brown paper parcel to me. 'This must be for you, Kat,' he said, 'there was a card sitting on top of it, addressed to "Kathlene".'

'But that's not my name,' I replied indignantly, though still taking the parcel.

'Well, it's close enough,' said Pop, shrugging. 'And Mom's name is Sarah, so it's definitely not for her. Why don't you open it and find out?'

Chapter Two

True Love's Hug

———

It occurred to me, of course, that there was only one person in the whole wide world who referred to me as Kathlene, and that was Grandma Finn who, by the way, I'd always thought of as being *ever so slightly* eccentric. She reckoned that I'd been given the wrong name at my baptism, and I should have been named Kathlene. She also said she was Wicca, and didn't believe in Christmas, Easter, or any other kind of celebration unless its name ended in "solstice". That's probably simplifying it way too much, but you get my drift.

So, unless someone had made a mistake and simply misspelled my name, the question was: why would Grandma Finn send me a present at all? Mom remained noticeably silent but, as you might expect, Pop came up with a totally different view on things.

He took the parcel and shook it. Hard.

'It's very light,' he said. 'It feels like an empty box.' He shook it again. 'I do wonder whether it's nothing more than a prank, maybe from one of your friends. That Marcas chappie, he was here overnight, I bet he hid it for a laugh. Come on, open it up, let's see if it's just a joke.'

Mom suddenly squealed. 'Yes,' she cried. 'It'll be a joke. Let's just put it in the bin, shall we?'

'Are you okay, Sarah?' Pop asked. 'You look as if *you've* seen a ghost. And we can't put it in the bin, not without finding out.'

'Pop is right about the parcel, Mom, there's only one way to find out what's in it.'

As I tore the wrapping off, Pop was looking over my shoulder, and burst out laughing when he saw what was inside. It was an old and tattered, plain green shoebox, on the lid of which were the letters *A R K*. Just below these, in faded gold lettering, it read, '*Augmented Reality for the Kurious*'.

I'm not really interested in all the nerdy tech stuff, so I had to ask Pop. 'What's Augmented Reality?'

Pop must have taken about ten minutes to explain it, all of which boiled down to the fact that some technology can superimpose computer generated images onto images of your actual surroundings. Impressive? No, I didn't think so, either.

'It must be a practical joke,' he said, still laughing. 'No real present would have Curious spelled with a K. Besides, there's nothing on the box apart from that. No branding, no serial number, nothing. Come on, open the box, let's see what's in it.'

I lifted the lid and peered inside. Wrapped in a piece of flimsy white paper was a blue headset with a white, adjustable strap. The headset was the kind that sits on your face like an overgrown pair of sunglasses. Taking it out, I turned it over and over in my hands. I knew what Pop had described it as, but there were no instructions and I couldn't even see how to turn it on. I handed it back to Pop.

'Let's see,' said Pop, as his chuckling stopped and he took on the fixed stare that he always had when confronted by a new gadget. He, too, turned it over and over, scratching his head as he did so. 'No,' he said after a few minutes, 'it's definitely a joke. There's nowhere to put batteries or plug it in. No buttons, no way of connecting it to the internet.' He handed the headset back to me. 'One of your friends must be sitting at home chuckling to themselves at your expense. Just Marcas my words. Get it, Kat? Marcas… my words?'

'You think you're funny, don't you Pop?' I teased him.

'I used to,' he sighed, 'before you came along.'

He handed the headset back to me. 'Seriously, though,' he said, 'if I were you, I'd ask Marcas about it. He's the only one who could have left it here.'

'It couldn't be him,' I replied, defensively, 'I know he gets into trouble sometimes, but he's also one of the most kind and genuine people you could meet. And he didn't mention anything about it when we were with him this morning.'

But however much I defended him, there was still a tiny smidgen of doubt in my mind. 'I'm going to phone him to make sure, though,' I said. Then I muttered under my breath, 'He'd better not have left this.' Pop laughed again, and went off to see how the coffee was progressing.

I was just going to put the headset down, so that I could phone Marcas, when I heard my name being whispered so quietly I thought I might have imagined it. Well, not actually *my* name as such.

'Kathlene.' It seemed to come from the ARK.

'What was that?' I asked, dropping the headset on the carpet.

'What was what?' said Mom.

'I heard my name. Bother, not my name, I heard the name Kathlene being whispered.'

'I didn't hear anything. You must be imagining it,' said Mom. She turned away, and I'm sure I heard her say to herself, 'at least, I wish you'd imagined it.'

Again, the whisper. 'Kathlene.'

'That's it,' I said, scooping it up. 'I'm going to phone Marcas. I'm going to get to the bottom of this. If he has left it as a joke, he'd better watch out. Not even my best buddy messes with The Kat.'

I phoned Marcas, who had only got back from Pets Corner about ten minutes earlier. He promptly denied sending presents to anyone at all, saying that he'd decided not to waste money buying things that people didn't really want or need. He did say, though, that he might be able to help with anything technical, so we arranged to meet by The Hooligoats' shed again.

—

As soon as I got to Pets Corner, I had that really weird feeling again, the feeling of being watched. It sent a cold shiver down my spine. I looked around once more, but couldn't see anyone. Everything was quiet. Which was odd in itself, of course. The parrots and ducks were silent, though they stood and watched me, as though they were expecting something to happen. Even the Kunekune pigs that lived in the next field along were quietly attentive.

While I waited for Marcas to show, I popped a fifty-pence piece into the gumball machine to get some linseed chips for The Hooligoats. As soon as I did that, the four of them came running from the other end of the field. This time, Ralph came right up to the fence, resisting Barney's attempts to push him out of the way. He stood on his hind legs and nuzzled his head into my open hand, bleating softly.

'I know, I know. I love you too, little one,' I murmured. 'And I really, really wish that I could understand what you're saying to me.'

Undeterred, Barney put his head down so that his horns were against Ralph's belly, and pushed harder at him. Ralph fell back onto all fours, and then he jumped up onto the wooden platform, his bleating getting much, much louder.

As you might expect, each of The Hooligoats had their own personality, and we'd given them nicknames to fit in with their character. Ralph had become known as Ralph the Raucous because he was usually such a noisy goat, whereas Barney was the Badass because he was such a, well, such a badass. Cuthbert had an especially lovely face, so he was known as the Cutie, and Fernando, who usually held back until he thought the situation was safe, was nicknamed the Fearful.

I put some treats onto the palm of my hand, and started to feed them, trying hard to give treats equally to each of them. This was not an easy task, because they all ran around excitedly, like mad things.

I'd almost run out of chips when there was a rustle in the trees behind me. I turned round, expecting Marcas to be there, but over by an elderflower bush was a tall figure dressed in a crimson-red cloak, which was pulled all around them and was so long it touched the ground. The hood was pulled up over their head, and I couldn't see a face at all, though I was sure there were red glows where the eyes would be. The figure spoke, its voice sounding oddly strained and weak. The hairs on the back of my neck began to prickle once more.

'I see the ARRRRK has found you,' said the voice quietly, then it threw its head back and yawped out a hideous sound like a cat being strangled. 'AHOOOOL,' it screeched, before its voice settled again. 'Wear it once, and you possess its gift forever, AHOOOOL.' An arm raised, and a long, bony finger pointed out at me. 'But heeeed my wooords. AHOOOOL. Only true love's kissss can bring you back to this life.'

You may think I'd have been frightened by this, but I honestly didn't feel scared, even if all the ahooooling was a bit unsettling. Having said that, I did struggle to come up with a meaningful retort, though I did the best I could.

'Er, I'm only eleven y'know, and I don't even have a boyfriend, not a proper one, anyway, so there's not going to be any of that "true love's kissing" going on.'

The figure hesitated, then glided towards me, appearing to hover gently in the air by my side. Bending down, it whispered, 'I wouldn't sssssssay this to jussssst anybody, dearie, AHOOOOL, but a nice hug from a good ffffffriend would probably do the job jussssst as well.'

With a final 'AHOOOOL' the figure glided back to the elderflower bush, the branches of which were waving frantically in the air, and just, well, disappeared. With a plopping kind of sound.

Yes, I know. Maybe you wouldn't have done it, but I am The Kat, remember? Nine lives and all that? And yes, I've heard the old saying that Kuriosity killed The Kat and you'd be right, over the past few weeks or so, it's come pretty close. But, despite everything that's happened, I'm still here to tell you about all this, aren't I? Besides, I couldn't resist.

I put the ARK on, adjusting it so that it fitted snugly over my eyes. There was a blinding flash of green light and everything went blurry. Gradually, things started to come back into focus, then…

'LOOK OUT!' cried a voice, as I could see Barney, with his two massive horns, charging towards me. He hit me hard, right on my forehead, and I went flying, landing heavily against the fence.

'Ow, ow, that hurt, you, you swine,' I shouted.

'Swine are in the next field along,' said Barney. 'Kunekune pigs to be exak.'

'Wow,' I cried. 'Either I'm dreaming or these glasses are really good. They actually make it seem like you talk.' I got up and turned round, only to find Ralph staring straight into my eyes.

'Apologies,' he said. 'Barney is always doing that.' He looked over at Barney. 'Say you're sorry, that's no way to treat a guest, especially when she's given us lots of treats.'

''Tis,' sneered Barney, 'and why is she pooping into our drinking water?'

I looked down, expecting to see normal legs, but instead, mine were short, covered in thick ginger fur and ended in… dainty little hooves.

Now, the thought of having hooves was a bit freaky. 'Er, okay,' I murmured. 'I've got dainty little hooves instead of feet. I think I need to get these specs off. Now.'

'Do you mean the headset?' asked Cuthbert. 'It's over there in the hay. It fell off after that flash of light.'

Before I could say any more, I noticed that Fernando was standing behind Barney, peering out at me.

'I'm not scared of her,' he muttered to the others. 'Really I'm not, but I've never seen a red pygmy goat before and that's one heck of a lot of poop.'

I followed his gaze and, sure enough, small round pellets were still tumbling uncontrollably from my hindquarters and into the water bowl.

'Sorry,' I said sheepishly.

'Don't worry,' giggled Ralph. 'Mr Gohturd will sort it out when he gets here. Though I don't think we should let him find you. He's only oooman, y'know, and he probably won't understand.'

I hate it when the huh gets dropped from the beginning of words.

'It's hhhhuman,' I scolded him, 'not oooman. You're not an "oooligoat", are you?'

'No, I'm a Hhhhooligoat.' He headbutted me playfully. 'And so are you.'

And then it dawned on me. If I *were* dreaming, Barney's headbutt wouldn't have hurt so much, and if the ARK was not on my head, then...

'Wait a minute, what did you say?' I shrieked. 'Oh no, I am a Hooligoat.' I ran round and round in circles until I was dizzy. 'What to do, what to do? Don't panic,' I shouted, as I collapsed into a pile of hay. The others stared at me, then fell about laughing. I glared hard at them until they stopped.

'Okay, keep calm and think. What did that, that ahooooly thing say? Ah, yes, true love's, er, hug. Oh, dear, and just how do we do that now? And why aren't there any of those ooomans around when you need one?'

Chapter Three

That's Just Weird!

I got up from the hay and shook myself.

'Eeuuwww,' I cried. 'I feel all itchy now. I hope there weren't any creepy crawlies in that hay.'

'Of course there are creepy crawlies,' replied Ralph. 'We goats live alongside lots of creepy crawlies. Most of them are very friendly.'

'Most of them?' I shuddered. 'Does that mean some of them are not friendly?'

'Don't worry about the bugs, Kat, they're all much smaller than we are. Look on the bright side,' continued Ralph, smiling. 'You said you wished you could understand what we're saying and now you can.'

'Yes, I know I can understand what you say, but that's hardly the point,' I said impatiently.

'So, what *is* the point?' asked Cuthbert.

'The point is,' I said, even more impatiently, 'the point is that I'm now a Hooligoat, and I'd like to get back to being oooman, er, I mean human.'

Barney gingerly stepped forward, with Fernando still peering out from behind him.

'Sorry,' he said apologetically.

'And what,' I said suspiciously, 'are you sorry for? Could it be sorry for laughing at me when I ran round and round and fell down?'

Fernando giggled. 'Oh, no. That was really, really funny. Please do that again.'

I glared.

'Er, no, perhaps not,' continued Barney, meekly. 'What I meant was, sorry for butting you when you first, sort of, arrived. I only did it because you startled me, y'know. So, sorry, again. We just don't tend to get many hhhhumans suddenly disappearing in a flash of light and re-appearing as one of us. Bit disconcerting.'

'Okay. Guys.' I looked round at them all. 'You don't need to keep emphasising the huhs. One huh is enough. Human, not hhhhuman. Right?'

I'm not sure why, but I stamped my hoof hard on the floor. Which hurt. There was another giggle from Fernando.

'Barney, thank you for apologising, and please don't headbutt me like that again. It really hurt. And, whatever you do,' I looked pointedly at Fernando, 'DON'T laugh or giggle at me again either, or I'll get very VERY cross.'

Fernando retreated even further behind cover, and I heard him whisper something to Barney.

'Fernie wants to know how you managed to do it. How you became one of us,' Barney said.

'Ah, I wish I knew, but it's a mystery. I have no idea,' I said, thoughtfully. 'I remember putting the ARK, the *Augmented Reality for the Kurious* headset on, there was a green flash and then… here I am, a Hooligoat. Which reminds me. I need to find that thing. Keep it safe.' I turned and looked round in the hay.

'It's gone,' said Cuthbert. 'While you were busy doing the falling down bit, there was a puff of smoke and off it went.'

'What's with all the smoke and flashes of light?' I asked, as a feeling of frustration began to bite at me. 'And don't tell me it's a magic thing.'

'Well, if you're not dreaming, and it's not your Augmented Reality doodah, I'm afraid it must be a magic thing,' said Ralph. 'After all, when you've eliminated the impossible, whatever remains, however improbable, must be the truth.'

I couldn't believe what I was hearing. 'You've read Sherlock Holmes? That's very intelligent of you,' I said.

Ralph looked at me as though my own intelligence wasn't up to much.

'Don't be silly, Kat Hooligoat, we can't read. But Mr Gohturd [Fernando giggled] sometimes sits over there on our bench and reads out loud. He likes a bit of detective stuff, and I think he gets a little lonely sometimes, when Bronwen is working in the café.'

I wasn't sure that goats being able to read was any more weird than me turning into one of them, but I thought it best to let it pass.

Ralph continued, 'And don't forget that the ahooooly thing told you that, once you wore it, you would have the ARK's gift forever.'

'So?'

'Well, if you have the gift forever, you don't need the ARK anymore.'

'Clever,' I muttered. 'I like the way you think. But I still need to get back to being human. Mom and Pop must be missing me by now. They'll be worried sick. And where, oh where, has Marcas got to? He should have been here ages ago.'

'Well, there's nothing we can do but wait for him,' suggested Ralph, as he began to walk back into the shed, making a beeline for the hayrack. 'And in the meantime, let's get some more hay. I'm hungry.'

'You're always hungry,' quipped Cuthbert, as he too wandered indoors.

–

Now, I know you'll be expecting me to tell you what it was like to be a pygmy goat. Well, *strange* is the first word that comes to mind. Definitely *strange*. All in all, though, it wasn't as bad as you might think. In fact, after a while, it seemed almost kind of natural, as though I was always meant to be one. And I love being able to talk with them. The creepy crawly thing bothered me at first. Obviously. And walking on four legs instead of two? That took some getting used to, I can tell you. Not so much, though, as the whole digestion stuff, which is seriously weird. I mean, apart from the spontaneous pooping, the fact that goats have four parts to their stomachs, instead of just one, seemed really bizarre to begin with. It took quite a time to learn that I could chew some hay, swallow it so that it goes into the first compartment, which is called the rumen, and then bring it back into my mouth to chew it some more. Apparently, this is called chewing the cud, or ruminating, and it totally grossed me out to begin with. And I certainly wouldn't recommend doing it at the dinner table. From experience, I can tell you that people tend to leave the room in something of a hurry when you start regurgitating food. Of course, it's also worth a mention that goats are herbivores, so don't eat meat at all. As I'd been vegetarian since I can remember, that suited me just fine.

–

Anyhoo, I followed Ralph and Cuthbert and watched as they both stood on their hind legs and pulled some strands of hay out of the rack with their mouths and promptly started to nibble it. Before they could get down onto four legs, however, Barney came striding in, with Fernando close behind.

'Make way for the Badass,' he shouted, and barged the other two out of the way.

'Hang on,' I cried. 'Hang on. That's what Marcas and I nicknamed you. What a coincidence.'

'No coincidensh, mish,' said Barney, his mouth full of hay. 'We undershtand evernink that humans say. No big deal.'

'Ah yes, of course you do,' I said. 'Ralph was just telling me about listening to Mr Gohturd.'

Fernando giggled. I gave him a sidelong glance before continuing.

'So do you like Conan Doyle too, Barney?'

'No, mish, *'Ungry Caterpillar* is more up my street.'

I ignored the missing huh. *'Hungry Caterpillar*? Is that one that he reads as well?'

'No, mish, little girl called Blodwyn comes along shometimes, with her mum. Nice girl. Pushes ush around a bit, but gives ush loads of treats.'

'You really love those linseed chips, don't you,' I muttered pensively. 'I must try one.'

Cuthbert swallowed his mouthful of hay, and looked innocently at me. 'Kat Hooligoat,' he said sweetly, 'ask Barney about when he thought Bossy Barbara was giving him a linseed treat. Go on, do ask him.'

'How was I to know?' demanded Barney.

Fernando stopped eating and joined in. 'It was during goat-yoga,' he said.

I'd never heard of that. 'Goat-yoga? That's a new one on me. What is it?' I asked.

'It's when people do yoga,' explained Ralph, 'and get into those really odd-looking positions. Then goats trample all over them. Humans do it because it's supposed to help get rid of knots in their muscles, but goats actually try to avoid the knots and put the hoof into more delicate areas.'

'Wow, you learn something every day,' I muttered. 'So you did goat-yoga with Mrs B?'

'Barney did. We think she chose him because he's heavier that the rest of us. Better for the knots.'

'Okay, okay, I'll tell her,' stormed Barney. 'You lot just make it up as you go along.'

'Come on then, Barney, what happened?' I asked soothingly.

'Well, Bossy does lots of yoga, says it keeps her trim despite her age. So, one day, she got Mr Gohturd [another giggle from Fernando] to take me to her house because one of her friends had said how good goat-yoga was and she wanted to try it.'

Barney looked uncomfortably bashful.

'And?' I prompted.

'Unfortunately,' he murmured, 'when she's at home by herself, she does *naked* yoga.'

I gasped at the thought. It wasn't a vision that I wanted in my head.

'I mean,' Barney went on, his top lip curling up in distaste, 'humans are not pretty to look at at the best of times, but that day still gives me nightmares. Especially because she got into positions that people are really not meant to bend themselves into.'

Ralph got impatient.

'But tell her about the linseed chip,' he urged.

'I'm coming to it, stop rushing me. So, yes, there was one position that she got into, while I was standing on her back, that meant her bum was sticking up in the air.'

'Oh, no,' I cried. 'I'm not sure I want to hear this.'

But there was no stopping Barney now.

'And when I looked at it, there was a linseed chip on top of her bottom.'

'Except it wasn't a linseed chip,' laughed Fernando excitedly.

Should I ask? Oh, dear, yes I did.

'So, what was it?'

'It was a boil,' shouted Cuthbert. 'She had a boil on her bum, and Barney bit it.'

Barney nodded and hung his head low.

'I was so agitated, and all that leaping around made me hungry.'

It took a while for the scene to sink into my brain. Once it was there, I couldn't get rid of it.

'Was she cross?' I asked, trying hard to suppress a horrified giggle.

'She reared up in the air, then came crashing down flat on the floor, and I fell off,' murmured Barney, sadly. 'Trouble was, her nose was then in the perfect position for a headbutt.'

'Oh, my. Poor Barney,' I croaked. 'So that's why she hates you all.'

–

After Barney had gone to lie down for a while, to get over the memory of his experience, Ralph looked at me thoughtfully.

'Are you interested in experiments?' he asked.

I should have known better.

'I suppose so,' I replied. 'So long as animals are not harmed in any way.'

'Strange you should ask that,' he said excitedly, 'but there's a project I've been working on.'

'Whoa,' I protested. 'I don't think I actually *asked* anything.'

'Ah, but in your mind you did.'

That was all I needed, a pygmy goat that could tell what I was thinking.

'That's just guessing, but okay, what's the experiment?' I said.

'Well,' said Ralph smugly, 'some time ago, I heard a conversation between Bossy Barbara and Mr Gohturd.'

Fernando giggled.

'Excuse Fernie,' Ralph sighed. 'He does that whenever he hears the name Gohturd.'

Another giggle.

Ralph sighed again. 'None of the rest of us understand why it's so funny.'

Fernando nudged into him. 'Why what's so funny, Ralph?'

'Gohturd,' replied Ralph.

'Ah, ha, ha, ha, ha, gotcha,' laughed Fernando. 'That is just so, so, so funny. Ha, ha, ha.'

'You behave like a little kid at times, Fernie. You can be so irritating.' Ralph turned back to me. 'Now, Kat, let me tell you about the conversation between Bossy Barbara and the-man-who-looks-after-us-who-shall-remain-nameless.'

'Er, I'm all ears,' I said.

Ralph looked at me strangely.

'Really?' he said. 'You're *all* ears?'

'Oh, for goodness' sake. I didn't mean that literally. Get on with it.'

'Okay, okay. Just checking. About the ears.'

By now, I was getting a little exasperated. 'Are you guys always like this?' I shouted.

'No,' said Barney, coming back to get some more hay. 'They're not usually so sensible, sometimes they can get a bit silly.'

I groaned. 'One last chance, Ralph. What-is-the-project?'

'Right, well, Bossy Barbara and the-man-who-looks-after-us-who-shall-remain-nameless were talking about the fact that she wanted to get rid of us so that she could open a farming museum. The-man-who-looks-after-us-who-shall-remain-nameless suggested that the lady at number nine might be able to house us. Then Bossy Barbara said, "Huh, and pigs might fly!" So,' Ralph ended with a flourish, 'there you have it.'

'There I have what?' I asked, really, really wishing I hadn't been so inquisitive.

'Well, flying pigs, of course. It's obvious isn't it? Why, as soon as she said that, I started to wonder how we could actually get pigs airborne. I mean, we have two in the next field who, I'm sure, are just desperate to join in with some boney fido research.'

'You have got to be kidding me,' I muttered.

'No, seriously,' Ralph insisted. 'All we need to do is feed them huge amounts of cabbage. Huge amounts. When they digest it all, it creates lots of gas in their stomach. Then, when they fart, *voilà*, they take off and we have jet-powered flying pigs. Admittedly, bringing them back down for a soft landing presents a bit of a problem but, as soon as I've figured that out, we're good-to-go.'

'Oh, no,' I cried. 'Oh, no. I honestly think I need to lie down. This is worse than Barney and the linseed chip.'

'So you're not keen on the—' started Ralph, but just then there was a shout from outside the shed. It was Mom.

'Kat. Are you in there, Kat?' she called.

I panicked. Well, wouldn't you panic if your mom was about to discover you'd turned into a pygmy goat?

'She mustn't see me like this,' I whispered to the others. 'I need to hide. Ralph, Fernando, you two go outside or she'll suspect something. And, whatever you do, don't let her come here into the shed. She'll die of shock if she sees me.'

'Why me?' whined Fernando. 'Why do I have to go out? Can't Cuthbert go?'

'For goodness' sake, Fernie,' grunted Barney. 'Just get on with it.'

'Kat,' shouted Mom again. 'It's okay, you can come out.'

'Go,' I whispered forcefully. 'Quickly.'

Ralph trotted out of the shed, with Fernando reluctantly plodding along behind him, head bowed. Barney, Cuthbert and I huddled up the in far corner of the shed, out of sight and hardly daring to breathe.

'Ralph,' we heard Mom coo affectionately. 'And Fernando. Lovely to see you both. Now, do you know where Kat is?'

'No idea,' bleated Ralph.

'Don't be stupid, Ralph,' scolded Fernando. 'She can't understand what you're saying. She's human, not like Kat.' There was a pause, then Fernando continued, in a mocking kind of voice, 'Actually, Mrs Briscoe, Kat is in the shed.' Then he giggled.

There was a *clump* sound as the two of them stood and put their front hooves on the fence.

'Ooooh, that's nice, Mrs Briscoe,' murmured Ralph. 'I do so love having my ears tickled.'

Mom's voice changed. 'I'm so glad you love having your ears tickled, Ralph,' she hissed. 'And yes Fernando, I can understand what you're saying. Every word. Now, go and tell Kat to come out here. OR ELSE.'

No-one knows quite why Fernando said it. We thought he must have taken a brave-pill.

'Or else, what?' he said, defiantly. Big mistake, as it happened.

Seconds later, Ralph burst back into the shed by himself and stood in front of us, shaking like a leaf.

'Er, where is Fernie?' I asked.

'He...' Ralph could hardly speak. 'He...'

'He what?' said Barney. 'Come on Ralph, pull y'self together, goat.'

Ralph took a deep breath. 'He passed out when he saw her,' he moaned. 'She may have eaten him by now.'

'When he saw who?' I asked.

'Your mom,' said Ralph who, by now, was just staring into space.

'My mom?' I said, confused. 'What about my mom?'

'She's turned into a...' Ralph muttered, 'she's turned into a...' he paused, trying to breathe, 'a Weirdwolf.'

'That's ridiculous, Ralph,' I scoffed. 'You're imagining things. And I think the term you're after is Werewolf.'

'I know what I mean,' he replied. 'Have you ever seen a wolf with curly blonde fur and strawberry-pink highlights?'

I peered outside through a crack in the doorway. There

was Mom, standing at the fence. I turned to Ralph.

'See? I told you that you were imagining it, you clot. My mom is human, and always has been.'

Mom shouted again. 'Kat, I can see you, you know. And, don't worry, I know all about you turning into a pygmy goat. Come on out, let's talk.'

'But how?' I muttered.

'Go on,' urged Barney. 'I think we all need to find out.'

I trotted out, stepping over Fernando, who was still lying spark-out by the fence, and stood in front of Mom.

'I'm sorry Mom,' I began, 'I don't know how I became a Hooligoat.'

'I know, dear. Don't worry about it,' she said, smiling broadly.

As I looked at her, my legs started to turn to jelly, and all four of my stomachs began churning. I could barely speak.

'Er, Mom,' I choked, trying to back away without taking my eyes off her.

'Yes, sweetie?'

'Erm, are those… fangs?'

Chapter Four

Don't Mention The...

O nce Mom had covered her mouth with her hand so that she could re-adjust her teeth, she turned to me. 'Ooops, dear, sorry about that. Actually, they're canine teeth rather than fangs. I'm not a snake, you know. Now, I reckon you might need a hug? Get back to being human?'

'Oh, yes please, Mom, a hug would be good, just so long as those canine fang things don't pop out again. You, um, you know all about this, then?'

'I do, unfortunately, yes. And by the time we get back home, Grandma Finn should have arrived. She's going to be staying with us for a time, so that she can go through everything with you right from the start. I think we owe you that much at least. But before we have a hug, just think for a while. This is your first time as a Hooligoat, so make sure you're ready to leave the other goats and go back to your human form.'

'Mom, are you joking?' I whispered. 'They've been telling me about their plans to turn the Kunekune pigs into rocket-propelled…' I was lost for words, 'rockets. These goats are completely mad. I can't wait to get back to being me.'

'But isn't that why we all call them Hooligoats, Kat? They're pygmy goats with serious attitude.'

I thought for a few moments and gradually calmed down.

'Actually, Mom, you're right, I've really enjoyed being a Hooligoat. I think I was just worried about changing back to being human and it was making me grouchy. Will I be able to be a Hooligoat again, then?'

'Of course, Kat. Now you've done it with help from the ARK, you should be able to do it by yourself. That's one of the things that Grandma will be helping you with. Now, say goodbye to the boys for now.'

I turned round in time to see Fernando struggling to his feet. He looked at Mom, then shrieked loudly and raced into the shed.

'I'll be back, lads,' I said fondly. 'Either as a human, or a Hooligoat. But I'll be back soon.'

'Bring us loads of linseed chips again next time, then,' shouted Ralph.

'Course I will. Bye everyone. Be good. And NO pig experiments, Ralph.'

Mom reached down and threw her arms around me in a big, big hug. There was yet another flash, and I looked down to see normal legs and feet.

'Time to go home,' Mom said.

We held hands and turned to make our way through the gate, only to find Pop propping himself up against a post, staring at us, his face white as a sheet.

'I think,' he said, 'I think I've seen my darling wife turn into a wolf and back again, and a Hooligoat being transformed into my daughter. Transformed, that is, by my darling wife who, in case I didn't mention it, happens to be a wolf. Trouble is, I don't think I *can* think. Not anymore.'

With that he fainted, crumpling up on the floor.

'Oh, bother,' muttered Mom. 'Looks like we're going to have to explain to your father as well. That's strictly against the rules.'

–

Getting back home was not easy at all. Mom didn't want to phone for an ambulance, for obvious reasons.

'No sense in letting him babble on to nurses about wolves and goats,' Mom explained, 'so we'll use the wheelbarrow that Mr Gohturd keeps behind the old greenhouse over there, and take him home ourselves. Oh, and just so you know, I telephoned Marcas after you left the house earlier. Told him you'd changed your mind about going to meet him. He didn't sound surprised.'

Taking Pop home in a wheelbarrow was easier said than done. Trying to keep his arms and legs from hanging over the sides of the barrow and scraping along the ground wasn't the easiest of tasks. By the time we got back home, he was starting to regain consciousness, which was a big help because it meant that he could manage, with a little assistance, to walk up the garden path to the front door. He still looked somewhat bewildered, and Mom had to do her best to stop him from talking out loud about what he'd witnessed. At last, though, we were inside, and we shuffled Pop into his favourite armchair.

'Now,' said Mom, 'I suggest you go and have a hot shower, Kat.'

'A shower?' I said. 'But I had one this morning.'

'True,' replied Mom, sniffing at the air. 'But you've spent time as a goat since then.'

'Oh,' I said, 'how gross. Maybe turning into a goat isn't such a good idea.'

Mom laughed. 'Don't worry,' she said, 'the more you practice at changing, the more control you'll have over smell.' She looked down, and pointed at my feet. 'And you'll bring fewer bugs back with you.'

I looked down in horror, just in time to see an earwig trying to make its way into my shoe. Mom crouched down, picked it up and carefully carried it outside before depositing it on the grass. 'That's where you belong, little beastie.'

Suddenly itching all over, I ran upstairs to my room, got undressed and put on a dressing gown, ready to go for a shower, and made my way along the landing and into the bathroom. I reached over to turn the shower on, and steam started to fill the room. Taking a piece of toilet paper, I wiped the condensation from the mirror so that I could pin my hair up, and suddenly I realised that I was not alone. There was a dark shape hanging from the light on the ceiling.

I screamed loudly, ran out of the bathroom and hotfooted down to Mom, who was in the kitchen.

'Mom,' I shouted. 'There's – there's a huge bat in the bathroom.'

Suddenly, there was a crashing noise from upstairs.

'Not again,' Mom sighed. 'Come with me, Kat.'

Mom ran up the stairs, with me following at a safe distance. She raced into the bathroom, where a familiar figure sat slumped against the washbasin.

'Grandma, you've done it again, haven't you? You've been hanging upside down as a bat, then forgotten to stand upright on the floor before changing back. I've told you so many times that light fittings won't stand your human weight. Look at the mess, we'll have to get a builder in. Come downstairs with me. And don't forget to put your teeth back in.'

Mom stormed back out, with Grandma trailing behind her.

'Well,' moaned Grandma, 'I couldn't help it. You know what my memory is like. Just thought it was a good way to say hallo. Show meself, y'know?'

Pop was at the foot of the stairs, tightly clutching the bannister.

'Did I hear someone mention bats?' he said weakly. 'And why do we sometimes need to get a builder in when Grandma Finn comes to stay?'

'Reginald, dear,' Mom took hold of Pop's elbow and steered him back into the living room, 'please rest for a while. We're all going to have a nice chat later on, so all will be revealed, quite literally as it were.'

Grandma seemed to be having difficulty in finding a seat, so Mom helped her to the settee.

'Don't worry,' Grandma said, probably more loudly than was necessary. 'I always takes time to get me eyesight back after being a bat for more than an hour or so.'

'But I thought,' I said, 'that bats had really good eyesight?'

She peered at me. 'They do,' she said, 'until they get to my age. It's not easy to find an optician that can make spectacles to fit over bat-ears. And hanging upside down for the reading-test can be a bit tricky. Those frames they use are heavy, they keep falling off.'

Pop roused again. 'So G-Grandma F-Finn is a bat?' he stammered.

At this point, Mom had obviously decided to take control. 'Everyone, please.' She clapped her hands. 'Listen to me.'

The room went silent. Apart from a slight whimpering sound coming from Pop.

'Thank you,' she said, amiably. 'Now, who would like a nice cup of tea?'

—

Let me tell you upfront that I wouldn't have put Grandma down for being able to turn into a bat. I mean, would you? But, as you'll spot when I tell you shortly about the 'reveal', it turns out she's actually no common-or-garden variety of bat. In fact, she definitely isn't something you want to get on the wrong side of. But, no, both Mom and Grandma Finn had kept everything secret, including from Pop. Grandma Finn only visited occasionally, and Pop was right, we did sometimes have to have the builders in to repair damage after she came to see us. I suppose I should have been more observant. Still, back to what I was telling you...

—

We had to wait until Pop had recovered his composure, and some of his sanity, before Mom placed dishes of crisps and other nibbles on the coffee table and sat us all down ready for the big talk.

'Is Reginald fully compost-mentis, then?' asked Grandma Finn in a hushed voice.

Pop obviously heard her and replied, 'It's compos-mentis, Grandma, compost is the decomposing heap of vegetation at the bottom of the garden. And, yes, I'm back to being of sound mind, thank you.'

'Good for you, young man,' sniggered Grandma. 'It wouldn't do to be a pile of dead cabbage, would it?'

'Er, no, it wouldn't.' I don't think Pop knew quite what to say. He isn't too keen on being called a young man. Says it doesn't go with his status as a Tax Inspector.

When everyone was settled, Mom stood in front of us and began the evening. It was obvious she was just a tad nervous.

'Right. Well,' she mumbled, 'thank you all for coming along, tonight.'

'Mom,' I reminded her, 'we do actually live here. Apart from Grandma, who has, quite literally, flown in to be with us.' I couldn't resist a chuckle at my own joke, even if it was inadvertent. Mom grimaced and gave me a hard stare.

'Enough of that,' she said, appearing to gain confidence. 'We have a lot to get through. Now, Reginald,' she looked at Pop, 'are you sure you're okay to listen to this? I don't like the thought of having to get the wheelbarrow out again.'

Pop's face went bright red.

'Oooh look at that for a colour,' cackled Grandma, gleefully. 'Maybe you could be a beetroot rather than a cabbage.'

'Grandma!' shouted Mom. 'For goodness' sake, let's get on with things or we'll be here 'till next week.'

'Sorry, you're right. This is a serious matter. We've never let anyone in on our stuff before.'

'Indeed. So, I'm just going to get it right out in the open. Kat, Reginald, we're not actually one hundred per cent human. Well, sorry. I mean that, Reginald, you are one hundred per cent human. Kat, you aren't.'

'Oh,' said Pop, obviously trying to come to terms with this revelation. 'I thought you were just witches, or some such like. After all, Grandma said she was Wicca.' He paused. 'So how much per cent human are you, then?'

'Well, it's debatable, as Grandma will explain later. The reality is that Grandma, me, and Kat are descended from a genetically modified line of Huldufólk.'

'Huldufólk?' Pop and I chorused together. 'Never heard of them.'

'Literally translated, Huldufólk means *Hidden People*, so the whole idea is that not many people, not many humans, know of our existence. Well, they know of our existence, but not what we are.'

'But, Sarah, we've been married for nineteen years,' protested Pop, 'so how come this is the first I'm hearing of it?'

'Actually, dear, we've been married for twenty-five years, and the Huldufólk Creed strictly forbids us from making our true selves known. Which means that you can never tell anyone at all. N-E-V-E-R. Now, I've completely forgotten what I was going to say, so perhaps it's time to hand over to Grandma, who will tell you about our history, and what being a Huldufólk is like. Grandma?'

Mom reached over to Grandma to help her up.

'It's okay, I can manage. Eyes are back to normal, now.'

Grandma stood in front of us while Mom took her seat.

'What your mom forgot to say is that we Huldufólk can each shape-shift into a specific animal. Kat, you changed into a pygmy goat today. My fault, sorry about that. Your mom transmogrifies into a Siberian wolf, and I'm just a silly old bat. Tee, hee, hee, hee, hee, hee...'

She laughed at her little joke until I thought she was going to be ill.

'Well, hee, hee, hee,' she continued after a while, 'I'm not Wicca. That's just a bit of a red herring. I'm actually a Brazilian vampire bat, so not so silly after all. In fact, both your mom and me could tear a person's throat out in no time at all.'

Pop was starting to glaze over again, and I wondered whether we needed to have the wheelbarrow on standby after all.

—

What I couldn't understand at that point was why could Mom and Grandma transform into such exotic creatures while I got to be a pygmy goat? The unfairness of me getting to be a Hooligoat instead of something that could 'tear somebody's throat out' was a tad peeving, so I put my hand up and asked. Apparently, when I went through the Huldufólk baptism, there was a second baby going through the same ceremony. Needless to say, Grandma was officiating, and she'd flown in as a bat, so couldn't see very well. You'll know where I'm going with this, won't you? Grandma mixed up the scrolls, and the other baby girl was baptised as Kathlene and got the ability to transmogrify into a Welsh gryphon. A Welsh gryphon! Half lion, half eagle, and big enough to tear several throats out with just one swipe of its claws. Or should that be talons? Or has it got both? Well, whether it has claws or talons, it's an amazingly fantastic creature, and instead of being one, I got to be Katherine the Village Goat. Thank you for that, Grandma.

—

'Anyhow, just so as I don't forget anything,' Grandma said, 'I've made a list, which I have in this pocket.' She fumbled around in her skirt. 'Or then again, maybe it's in this pocket. No, try this one. Ah, got it.'

She held the list up, and I shuddered at the length of it, as it unfurled all the way down to the floor. We'd be there all night, I thought.

'First item,' said Grandma studiously examining her list. 'Oh, that one's just a reminder so, onto the next item then.'

I settled in and made myself comfortable. This was going to be a long night, by the looks of it. Of course, I wouldn't have been nearly so comfortable if I'd known that the first item on the list, the one that she'd said was just a reminder, was;

Item 1. Don't mention The Prophecy to Kathlene.

Chapter Five

Elves, But Not as We Know Them

———

I don't want you to get the impression that I resented being a pygmy goat rather than a gryphon. I have so enjoyed being a Hooligoat over the past few weeks. In between the life-threatening stuff, that is. But I think when I sat there, listening to Grandma that night, it did occur to me that being half lion, half eagle would have suited me down to the ground. In reality, of course, what I really wanted was to be able to transmogrify into either a goat, or a gryphon, depending on how I felt. I remember thinking at the time that would have been super cool. By the way, don't you think that *transmogrify* is a fantastically wonderful word?

–

Grandma's presentation did go on for a while and I think I may have dozed off a couple of times. After all, it had been something of a strange and tiring day, with one surprise after another. So, rather than relate everything that Grandma said, let me tell you what I think are the most important bits;

Firstly, the ARK wasn't sent by anyone. Apparently, no-one really understands what it is, or where it is from. We only know that it has a life of its own and has existed for as long as Huldufólk have, which is a very, very, very long time. Grandma thinks it's the ARK that's responsible for producing the scroll that's used at our baptisms, the scroll that determines what animal we can transmogrify into. It's at that point that it forms a bond with the baptisee. Then, when it judges that the time is right, it materialises as a gift for whichever Huldufólk girl is about to 'come of age'. And, of course, it doesn't always turn up as an *Augmented Reality for the Kurious* headset, but appears to try to keep up with technology. So, when Mom was a youngster, it came to her as an *Autonomous Reading Komputer* (a bit like an early version of an e-reader, storing digital books so you could enjoy a story without having to carry lots of physical books around). Grandma couldn't remember what it was for her, but I'm not sure technology was invented when she was young. The important thing about the ARK, though, is that it only needs to be used once to, kind of, kick-start the transmogrification process. Once that's done, it moves on to the next candidate.

Secondly, the screechy AHOOOOLY thing is actually Grandma's Familiar. Very like a witch's Familiar, which I think is a demon or spirit in the form of an animal, a Huldufólk's Familiar is an animal that can be transformed into a near-human form. In Grandma's case this happens to be, believe it or not, a koala bear that goes by the name Gertie. Now, you may think koalas are cute and cuddly critters, and you'd be right. The noise they make, however, is nothing short of horrendous especially when, as in Gertie's case, they are the size of a person. And they're also very loud. I understand they have an extra pair of vocal cords at the back of the nasal passage. If you get the chance to listen to one, don't forget your earplugs.

Thirdly, our particular line of Huldufólk came about hundreds and hundreds of years ago, after genetic experiments were carried out on regular Huldufólk by a scientist by the name of Dr Francine Nevaeh Steiner. Original Huldufólk were a race of elves, native to Iceland. Strictly speaking, I suppose, although we are still elves by nature, we should refer to ourselves as GM Huldufólk, though I'm not really comfortable with that expression. We always try to avoid anything that's been genetically modified, so to find out that I'm GM myself is a tad unsettling. Maybe the phrase Huldufólk 2.0 works better. Grandma was vague about the details, but it seems there was some cross-breeding going on that resulted in us being human for most of the time, and then able to shape-shift into our designated animal when we want to. I have no idea why, but whatever animal we can become is chosen for us and set out in our baptism ceremony. I also have no idea why we started off in Iceland and ended up in a small village near Dudley. I must remember to ask Grandma about that. Oh, and our magical powers became upgraded, which means that we no longer need to bother with reciting spells and incantations, though they don't usually kick in until later in life and use of them is heavily regulated by the Huldufólk Creed.

Several hundred years after her experiments on Huldufólk, Dr Steiner carried out various other experiments using her preferred name Dr Frankie N Steiner. Although Grandma says she has no idea where Dr Frankie lives now, she says that she turns up every now and then, but in a different body. Like *Doctor Who*, I suppose, though she's not fictional, and definitely not a Time Lord (or should that be Time Lady?). Sounds a bit wacky, doesn't it?

Next, our line is only through females. Huldufólk women have children with human males, but only daughters are produced. And every daughter goes on to develop Huldufólk abilities, including being able to understand what animals are saying, so maybe Dr Doolittle should make way for the experts! Oh, and all of us are either vegetarian or vegans when we're in human form. Something to do with respecting other animals, being as we can transmogrify into one. Interestingly, there is some debate about whether we should also be vegetarian whilst we're in our animal form. It's not a problem for Huldufólk like me, who change into herbivore-types, but Mom says she's really conflicted about what to eat when she's in wolf-form, and prefers to go hungry until she's back to being human. Good news for Ralph and Fernando...

Lastly, there is the aforementioned Huldufólk Creed. This sets out what Huldufólk can, and can't do, and is maintained by a governing body called The Elders.

Grandma had forgotten where she'd put my copy of the Creed, and promised to give it to me later. I'm still waiting, by the way. I have a feeling it doesn't really exist, and Grandma makes up the rules as she goes along…

I think that pretty much covers everything, so I'm not sure why it took Grandma more than two hours to run through it. Oh, one more thing I should mention. She said there's a problem with Global Warming. Now, we all know there's a problem with Global Warming, even though some people won't admit it, but Grandma clammed up when I asked her whether she had a specific problem in mind. It was as though she realised she shouldn't have mentioned it.

~

Going to sleep that night was difficult, even though Grandma made a cup of her special herbal tea for me. I kept having the feeling that I was a Hooligoat again, standing on piles of hay that had loads of creepy crawlies in. When I'd been with The Hooligoats earlier that day, I hadn't been brave enough, or hungry enough, to try to eat some hay. That was to come the following day. Yum…

Once I'd managed to fall asleep, I know that I dreamed lots. Again, it was mainly about being a Hooligoat, playing on the slide and the trampoline inside their pen, running round and round and gambolling about. In one dream, though, I think Ralph's 'flying pigs' project got to me, because I dreamed I had climbed onto the top level of the wooden platform that stood alongside their shed and jumped off. Instead of falling and landing safely on the ground, I started kicking my hooves about madly. All of a sudden, I was climbing up into the sky and my front legs had become giant wings, beating easily and gracefully in the air. I flew around for a while, then spotted some figures down below in a field. I swooped down and the next thing I knew I was 'tearing some throats out'. I woke up at that point sweating profusely. I never told Mom or Grandma about that dream. Or the fact that, when I woke up, there were a few feathers on the floor by my bed.

Chapter Six

All Change

———

Next morning, Pop had almost returned to his normal self. If you could have called Pop normal at any time, of course. As I went downstairs, he was whistling away, making breakfast. He looked up as I entered the kitchen.

'Mornin' Kat,' he said happily. 'How're you today? You must have had a very hectic day yesterday, what with becoming a Hooligoat and everything. Bit of a shock that was. Still, I always say that we are what we are, and best to make the most of it.'

I wasn't expecting him to be in such a good mood, but he assured me I wasn't still dreaming.

'So, what would you like for breakfast, then. Are you still vegetarian, even though you can turn into a goat?'

'Yes Pop, I'm still vegetarian, as are goats, of course. Mushrooms on toast would be great, thank you.'

'Grandma and Mom are going to take you back to Pets Corner today, they tell me. Teach you how to, what do you call it when you turn into a Hooligoat?'

'Transmogrify?'

'That's the one. What a lovely word it is.'

As soon as I had smelled the mushrooms sizzling away, I felt ravenously hungry, so when he laid my plate in front of me, I ate as though I hadn't eaten for weeks. While I was troughing, Mom and Grandma walked in.

'Glad to see you're eating well, Kat,' said Mom, 'we've got a busy day ahead of us. Oh, and we've arranged the party for the beginning of next month.'

'Party? What party?' I asked.

'The Coming Out party. For you and Kathlene. Or Katherine. Oh, I do get confused with this. The other girl. The one who got your name because someone couldn't be bothered to get the scrolls in the right order.' She gave a sidelong glance at Grandma, who blushed.

'I didn't know we had parties for Coming Out,' I said.

'Of course we do, it's an especially important point in your life. We've invited quite a few Huldufólk ladies and their daughters, so you'll be able to talk to some older girls who've been able to transform for some time. Learn from their experiences, so to speak. And you all get to show off your skills at transmogrifying when we get to the Parade.'

'Are there any others that change into pygmy goats, then?' I asked, hopefully.

'Er, no. Not exactly, no. There's one with a personality issue. She changes into a Siamese cat that thinks it's a dachshund, but not one that's a goat. Sorry.'

'And the girl who got to be a gryphon. Kathlene. She'll be at the party?'

'Joint Guest of Honour.'

'Hmmm.'

–

An hour later Mom, Pop, Grandma and I were all back at Pets Corner. It was much colder than on the Sunday, so I wasn't too keen on relying on the fur of a pygmy goat to keep me warm. In case you don't know, pygmy goats originate from West Africa, so we do like a bit of warmth. The Hooligoats, despite the weather, gathered expectantly at the fence near where we stood. As they'd requested, I'd garnered lots of fifty-pence coins so that we could raid the gumball machine for linseed chips.

Although the other three waited patiently, Ralph the Raucous was even more vociferous than usual.

'Come on, Kat, you can do it,' he shouted, though alternating with, 'where's the treats, then?'

After buying eight lots of treats, and feeding the obviously starving Hooligoats, my big moment arrived. Both Grandma and Mom had talked me through how to transform into a different animal without the aid of the ARK, so I had a good idea of what I needed to do. It couldn't be that difficult, could it? There were twelve Huldufólk girls coming to my party soon and, if they'd mastered it, I was sure I could.

'Don't forget,' said Grandma encouragingly, 'focus on one of the goats, and just visualise yourself becoming one. The first time will be a slow transformation, but you'll speed up with practice.'

So that's exactly what I did. Well, almost exactly. I stared really hard at Cuthbert, who fidgeted and whined under such an intense gaze. The problem was, I couldn't get the thought of being a gryphon completely out of my mind. I tried as best I could and then, just as I thought I couldn't do it, everything suddenly started to happen. I felt my legs getting shorter, my fur beginning to sprout, tail popping out at the rear and my horns extending out of the top of my head. I was exhilarated.

'I've done it, I've done it!' I shouted excitedly.

The goats gasped, and took a few steps backwards. 'Ooooh, nasty,' they all cried.

'Right,' said Grandma, sternly. 'Well, I don't know where your head was, but it certainly wasn't on becoming a goat. Good job we didn't bring a mirror.'

She clicked her fingers, and I instantly went back to being a girl. 'Now,' she said, a little more forcefully than I thought necessary. 'CONCENTRATE. A goat body with a girl's head just don't look right. Especially when the head has got horns sticking out the top, and goat ears popping out at the side.'

I think my face went the same colour as my hair. I composed myself and forced the image of a gryphon out of my head. This time, Cuthbert hid behind the others, so I focused on Ralph instead. All of my thoughts seemed to merge into one as I stood there, I didn't feel any elation. Just a gradual feeling that I'd like to try some hay.

'Well done, Kat Hooligoat,' shouted Ralph. 'Time for more treats, now.'

'Yes, well done, Kat. You're one of us again,' cried Cuthbert and Barney.

Fernando giggled nervously, still keeping an eye on Mom.

'There you go,' said Grandma with a sigh. 'I knew you could do it. All you have to do now is wait a few minutes and then change back to being a girl.'

'Okay,' I said calmly. 'But can I try some hay first?'

–

After I'd gone from girl to goat and back again four more times, Grandma was happy enough to call a halt for the day. I'd tried some hay, which I thought was tasteless, and even had one of the linseed chips. I could certainly understand why goats love them so much.

I'd spent some time talking with The Hooligoats, who all said they were very impressed with my ability. They wanted me to stay for longer, and I would have liked to, but I felt exhausted. Everyone, including Pop, who only looked slightly pale this time, agreed that I should return the next day, for more practice.

As we started to walk away, back towards home, I stopped dead in my tracks. Mom and Grandma looked at me oddly as I turned to gaze at The Hooligoats. Pop didn't notice and carried on walking. That's Pop for you.

'Grandma,' I said quietly. 'Grandma, can I ask you a question?'

'Technically, Kat,' she replied with a smile, 'you just did ask me a question.'

'Don't be awkward, Grandma, I need to know something.'

'In that case, of course you can ask a question.'

'It's just that, well, you know you have a Familiar, and you can make it appear as a human?'

Grandma had a slightly suspicious look on her face as she replied, 'My koala bear, Gertie, yes. But they can never be made perfectly human, they have at least one if not more, let's say, discrepancies. What of it?'

'Well, my question is, if you have a Familiar, but Mom doesn't have one, there can't be any rules in the Creed about how many Familiars we're allowed, can there?'

'I don't think so. Do I need to find out?'

Grandma suddenly seemed to know what was going through my mind. She looked at me, eyes opening widely, and then stared at The Hooligoats.

'Oh, my goodness,' she gasped. 'Are you thinking of having *four* Familiars? Are you sure having Barney transformed into human form would be a good idea? He isn't nicknamed the Badass for nothing, y'know.'

I nodded enthusiastically. 'He can't be all that bad,' I said. 'He actually apologised to me yesterday.'

Grandma breathed deeply. 'Then I think I should contact the rest of The Elders. See what they think.'

I laughed. 'Technically, Grandma, you can't *see* what someone thinks.'

'Oh, I wouldn't be too sure of that,' said Grandma.

Chapter Seven

The Prophecy,
and How to Avoid it...

———

L isten, quickly, Kat has just popped out for a while.
I know that she has started telling you about the
past few weeks but I thought that, as her mother, I
should mention something to you while she's not here. It's
a confession, I suppose. One that I'd like to make before she
gets to tell you any more, especially about what happened
at the Coming Out party.

You see, as with you humans, we Huldufólk have a
number of laws that govern the way we live. One of the
most serious ones is that no-one, other than a member of
The Elders such as Kat's grandma, may read The Prophecy.
Most of us know of its existence, but it has been closely
guarded by The Elders, and to read it is a crime that is
considered to be of the worst kind.

But I have to tell you, when I was just a child myself,
I sneaked a look at it while Grandma, my mom, was out.
I know I shouldn't have, I know if anyone had found out

I would have been in such terrible trouble, but I couldn't help it, it was almost as if The Prophecy was calling to me.

I only had time to read a small part of it, of course, but I remember so well what was in it. Like the fact that great evil would be resurrected by the deeds of mankind. And a Huldufólk child *with hair the colour of fire* would have the potential to harness the power of Mother Earth. She would lead our people against the evil.

So, when Kat was born, I wanted so much to protect her. I didn't want her to be caught up by such bad things, not my little girl. It wasn't her grandma who got the scrolls mixed up at the baptism. It was me. I deliberately gave Grandma the wrong one. Kat ended up getting the wrong name, and only being able to transform into a pygmy goat. After all, I thought, what harm could she come to as a goat? And then, of course, I did my best to prevent the ARK from finding Kat. After using a spell that I thought would confuse it, so that it couldn't sense where she was, I secured the house and made sure there was no way in. But I should have known there was no way of stopping it.

Oh, dear, there's more I should say, but she's coming back. It's probably best if you don't tell her what I've been saying.

Chapter Eight

A Visitor?

—

When we got back home, Grandma asked to use the phone so that she could contact The Elders about how many Familiars we're allowed to have. Pop offered his mobile phone for her to use, but she wouldn't take it.

'I'm not using one of those carry-it-about phones. Don't trust 'em.'

'It's called a mobile, Grandma, and they're perfectly safe.'

'Not in the hands of cousin Ada, they're not. She keeps dropping them down the toilet. I'm not touching one after that. Plugged-in phones. Can't drop those in a pile of poo.' Grandma's voice got a little louder, more insistent. 'Besides, Reginald, carry-it-about phones use lots of rare minerals. All the time, Mother Earth's resources are plundered just for the sake of people's convenience.'

How many times had I said almost the exact same thing to Pop, only for him to justify it by telling me that *everyone* has a mobile phone?

This time, though, Pop didn't say anything.

—

Half an hour later, just before we were about to sit down to supper, Grandma came back into the room and called for silence.

'Right, Kat. The answer is that no Huldufólk has ever had more than one Familiar. The Elders have no objection in principle, but they have voiced concerns about whether you'd be able to control four of them, especially four goats that are renowned for being mischievous at best, and dangerously reckless at worst. And you know I told you that Familiars have imperfections when they're turned into human form?' I nodded. 'Well, we think that having more than one Familiar would increase the number of imperfections that each of them has. So, they may look people'ish but, for instance, they may also have to wear a hat to disguise horns. Having said that, The Elders have agreed to discuss the matter further, and to let us know their decision in due course.'

'But Grandma,' I said, 'aren't you one of The Elders? Don't you need to be part of the discussions?'

'I've already given them my vote.'

'And are you going to tell me what you voted?'

Grandma pointed a finger and touched the end of my nose affectionately. 'Nosey is as nosey does,' she said.

'That's just not fair,' I protested. 'I don't even know what that means.'

'Nor me,' she laughed, 'but it sounded good at the time. Now let's eat supper. I'm starving, what about you?'

I nodded. 'So long as it's more tasty than hay.'

–

After supper, the four of us sat in the living room and chatted about the events of the day. I sat next to Pop, who was really being very understanding about the whole thing, though he did keep referring to Huldufólk as 'Dudleyfolk'. Understandable, I suppose, being as he comes from Oakham, just on the outskirts of Dudley.

Grandma, bless her, said she thought the whole thing was going very well, and that I was making good progress. She also thought we should go back to the goats again the next day, and the next day, and keep practising transmogrifying until I could do it almost without thinking.

I loved being a Hooligoat, of course, so the idea that we should spend time with them every day sounded perfect. Interestingly, Grandma also told us that The Elders had decided that, as Pop already knew the secret about Huldufólk, he should be able to help us where he could, and they even suggested that he could learn Hoolispeak. Pop was so happy about that. I think he'd dreaded being shut out from what we were doing.

As it happened, though, the next week was disrupted by awful weather. It was unseasonably cold, and it felt like there was one storm after another. Parts of the country had so much rain that people were trapped by flooding, and the wind blew, and blew, and blew. Grandma and I tried to go round to Pets Corner on the following day but the lane outside, which was lower than the fields that flanked it, was badly flooded, and Grandma decided we shouldn't risk trying to wade through to The Hooligoats. The farmhouse and the animal sheds were all at a higher level, and I knew from experience that the goats hated rain, and would do anything they could to avoid getting wet, so we thought they'd probably stay in the shed, keeping warm and dry.

Nonetheless, we climbed the bank at the side of the lane, peered over the hedge, and spotted Mrs Bradbury, dressed in a black hooded raincoat and green wellies, about to go into the farmhouse. She still had the pitchfork pointing forward.

'She must love that pitchfork,' I muttered.

Grandma chuckled, then shouted out, 'Hoo, hoo, Mrs Bradbury, coooey.'

I couldn't help but snigger. Fancy saying "coooey" to Bossy B.

She stood the pitchfork on the end, with the prongs pointing upwards, turned and looked at us.

Grandma shouted again. 'We just wanted to check that the goats were okay, given the bad weather an' all.'

Mrs B put on her poshest voice. 'Yes, those little horrors are fine, unfortunately.'

When she said that, I couldn't hold back the image of a naked Bossy Barbara doing contortions and having a boil on her bum being bitten by Barney. It certainly occurred to me that Barney's nickname *Badass* was highly appropriate.

'I'm having to look after all of the animals, y'know. Most inconvenient. That Gohturd man phoned to say the roads in his village are flooded and he can't get through. You'd think he would at least make the effort. When I was his age, I'd be up at the crack of dawn no matter what the weather was like, milking the cows, feeding the pigs, collecting eggs from the chicken run, all before stopping for no more than five minutes to have breakfast.'

'But,' I protested, 'his village is worse than this one for flooding. I'm sure he'd get through if he could.'

'Nonsense, girl. He's got wellington boots, hasn't he? I mean, don't get me started on work-ethics. The trouble with people these days is that they have no work-ethics. They're work-shy more like. Not like me in my younger days. Strong as an ox I was. Of course, after giving up the farm, I built Pets Corner by myself. No help from anyone. And when I was running it, all by myself, I'd have to look after the animals, and bake all the cakes, pastries and pies for the café, which I also ran single-handedly. At least I did until I decided, purely out of the goodness of my heart, to help that Bronwen woman out by giving her a job in there. And how does she repay me? By taking holidays, that's how. I never took holidays, not when I ran everything all by myself. No, people are just work-shy these days. And schools? Don't get me started on what schools are like these days. I expect they'll all stay closed next week because of the weather. Slightest excuse. Spineless, the lot of them. No doubt you'll be running amok, young lady, feeding those so-called Hooligoats instead of going to classes. And don't get me started on those vile goat-things. Honestly, I really wish I'd never agreed to have the beastly little animals here. I'll be glad when they've gone, I've got a number of recipes for Bronwen to try when the time comes. It'll be a meat-eater's paradise, so those vegan-people will just have to find somewhere else to eat. Oh, and I mean, don't get me started on vegans. Gohturd is a vegan. I just don't understand people today. Why would they be more interested in the wellbeing of a lamb than they are in the welfare of a farmer. Hmm? Tell me that. Why would they want to see a lamb mucking about, running around a field, but not want to see it on their dinner plate? Doesn't make any sense at all.'

Not wanting to 'get her started' on anything else, especially as she didn't even seem to know that school was already closed because term had ended, we made our excuses and left Mrs Bradbury, who stood the pitchfork up by the farmhouse door and went inside, muttering loudly under her breath. I'm sure she didn't know that Bronwen, who did all of the cooking at the Pets Corner café, and Mr Gohturd were actually living together, they were 'an item' as Pop would say. Not only were they living together, but they were also both vegans and both of them adored The Hooligoats, so I felt safe in the knowledge that Bronwen was highly unlikely to agree to cook the lads, no matter what recipe Mrs Bradbury wanted her to use.

–

As we made our way back home, Grandma chuckled to herself. 'I can understand why The Hooligoats think the goat-yoga incident was so funny. I reckon they'd love to trample all over her.'

'Goat-yoga? How did you know about that, Grandma?' I asked.

'Gertie told me.'

'Your Familiar?'

'S'right,' explained Grandma. 'After telling you about the ARK, she hung around for a while, so that she could just keep an eye on things until your mom got there.'

'Where is Gertie now? Does she live in your room?'

'Oh, no. She's away on a mission.' Grandma was thoughtful. 'D'yer know, listening to Bossy Barbara, it occurred to me that if she knew what I was doing when I was younger, it would make her toes curl until they reached her ankles.'

I couldn't help being curious. 'Really, and what was that?'

'Oh, I'll tell you one day, when the time is right.'

'Grandma, that is so frustrating,' I cried. 'And I've just realised that I don't actually know how old you are. Would it be rude of me to ask?'

'No, I don't mind you asking. Truth is, I'm as old as I want to be.'

I laughed. 'You mean you're as old as you feel. Pop is always saying that.'

'No, Kat, I know exactly what I mean, and I really mean I'm as old as I want to be. At the moment, it suits me to be this age. Otherwise I wouldn't look right as your grandma. But, when you're grown up, and don't need me around anymore, I might choose to be a different age. Perks of being Huldufólk.'

'Grandma,' I said, slipping my arm through hers, 'I think I'll always want you around.'

She turned her head and smiled at me. It wasn't a happy smile.

'There's bad things coming, Kat. Bad, bad things.'

Grandma scared me sometimes. 'How bad?' I asked.

'As bad as it can be. I don't know exactly what it is, but Mother Earth is trembling. She's afraid. I can feel it.'

'I can't feel anything.'

'That's because you're not tuned in to it. Not yet. But you will be. You'll have no choice but to be tuned in. Otherwise, well, it don't bear thinking about.'

'But you're worrying me now, Grandma. How will I know when I'm tuned in?'

'Oh, you'll know, all right.'

'Okay, so describe it to me. What will happen?'

Grandma stopped and turned to me. 'Tell me, how do you know anything about the world around you?'

'Well. I suppose I can see what's happening.'

'With your eyes, yes. Your ability to see is the main sense that you use. But it's not the only one. So, what else?'

'I can hear, and smell stuff. Though some things I'd rather not smell.'

'And?'

'I can touch things. Oh, and I can taste.'

'There you go, then. Those five senses are the ones that most humans have. But Huldufólk have another one, a sixth sense.'

'Wasn't that a film about a boy who could see dead people? Pop loves that movie.'

'Don't be silly, Kat. This is serious. Our additional sense is one of being connected to everything around us, like being a computer that can read all of the internet all at the same time. When Mother Earth allows your sixth sense to kick in, you'll know about it. If it's not too late, that is.'

She smiled again. Brighter this time.

'Don't take any notice of me, Kat. I do talk some rubbish, sometimes. I just need a cup of tea and a biscuit.'

I wasn't convinced.

–

By the time we got back home we were both wet through, so it was nice to get back into the warm and dry. After changing into fresh clothes, we went through into the living room and Grandma sat on the settee.

'Time for a nice cup of tea and a biscuit,' she said loudly.

'Just one biscuit?' Mom shouted through from the kitchen.

'Best bring the packet through. Just in case. You know I gets peckish.'

'Good job I stocked up when you arrived, then.'

After a few minutes, Mom walked in with a tray bearing mugs of tea and a plate full of assorted biscuits.

'I presume you didn't manage to get through to the goats, then, being as Kat hasn't got any hay stuck in her hair,' Mom said.

Grandma answered, 'We had a one-sided chat with Bossy Bradbury instead. Interesting woman, that one. I have a feeling she's going to be trouble.' She winked at me. 'Might need to deal with her. One way or another.'

I turned to Mom. 'Where's Pop?' I asked.

'Oh, he's been learning a bit of Hoolispeak while you were out,' answered Mom, 'so he's upstairs, practising.'

A thought suddenly occurred to me.

'Can I ask you another question, Grandma?' I asked.

'Course you can.'

'Well, I know Pop is learning goat language, but do all goats speak the same language? I mean, if a goat lives in France, does it speak French goat language? And what about German or Dutch goats?'

'That's a very, very intelligent question, Kat. Well done for thinking of it,' said Grandma.

'And the answer is?'

'I have no idea. I've never been abroad, so I wouldn't know.'

'What, never?'

'Nope. Been to Scotland once on a business trip, which was a bit messy. And Wales, that was nice. Had some lovely times in Ireland. Very green. I've even done lots of visits to Dudley Castle, which is just along from where I live. Do you know, they have the world's largest collection of Tecton structures in the grounds of the castle?' I shook my head. 'Anyhoo,' continued Grandma, 'I've never met a French goat, so I have no idea what language they speak. Ask Ralph or Cuthbert, they may know. 'Sides, The Hooligoats definitely were born in this country, so your dad only needs to understand what they are saying.'

'What are Tecton structures?'

'You're full of questions today, aren't you? I'll show you some photos of them later. Fascinating things they are.'

–

After the cup of tea, complete with almost the whole plateful of biscuits, Grandma said she wanted to have a lie down and a think. She was just going through the door when Pop came downstairs.

Grandma bleated at him.

Pop beamed. 'Oooh, er. Hang on, I know that one, we've just done it,' he said enthusiastically, then he bleated back to Grandma.

'Well done, young man,' she said approvingly, and went upstairs.

Pop came in, a smug look on his face, and looked at the empty mugs and the plate. Then came the words I dreaded.

'There's a fair bit of washing-up in the kitchen, as well, Kat.'

Mom and Pop both looked at me, so it wasn't easy to say no. All I could manage was, 'If we had a dishwasher, it would be so much easier.'

'We *have* got a dishwasher,' they both said in chorus. 'She's called Kat.'

The two of them laughed. I could even hear Grandma chuckling away upstairs. I didn't think it was that funny.

'Here's a question though Mom,' I retorted. 'If you and Grandma have magical powers, why can't you use those to get the washing-up done?'

'Strictly forbidden in the Creed, I'm afraid, Kat. And you only have to read *The Sorcerer's Apprentice* to understand why.'

They still sat looking at me, so off I went to the kitchen. At least Pop helped to carry the mugs out.

'Give me a shout when you've done some,' he said, smiling, 'and I'll come and dry things. It'll be quicker with two pairs of hands rather than one.'

As Pop went back to the living room, I made a start, washing the dishes which were the least dirty first. It didn't take long to amass a pile of them on the draining board, waiting to be dried. I took my rubber gloves off, and was about to go and call Pop when I realised that something wasn't quite right. I stood and stared through the kitchen window.

It was already almost dark outside. Rainclouds were racing across the sky, blown by powerful winds, which gusted so strongly at times that trees and bushes were bending over, their branches shaking wildly. In the poor light, it was difficult to see clearly but, in the centre of the garden, there appeared to be some kind of figure. I couldn't see any features, other than two pale pinpoints of light. As soon as I caught sight of it, it disappeared.

I decided at the time that it wasn't worth mentioning to Grandma or Mom, I thought it must have been a trick of the light and the weather. Or maybe it was Gertie.

What a mistake that turned out to be.

Chapter Nine
Police Come Knocking

‎—

The next day started badly. Very badly.

I was about to go downstairs from my bedroom when the doorbell rang. I heard Pop coming out of the kitchen, muttering to himself about people disturbing him at breakfast time. I'm not sure why, but I moved around the landing so that I couldn't be seen from downstairs. Pop unbolted the front door and opened it. A woman spoke.

'Good morning, sir. You are Mr Reginald Briscoe?'

'Yes, what of it?'

'I'm Detective Chief Inspector Doune. Vera Doune, sir, West Midlands Police. This lady is Detective Sergeant Wiles. May we come in?'

'Yes, of course. What's all this about?'

Grandma came out of her room and looked at me, finger pressed firmly against her lips.

'This can't be anything to do with us, can it Grandma?' I whispered. 'They can't know about us, can they?'

Grandma whispered back, 'I don't see how they'd know, Kat, we've been very discreet. Let's listen.'

The two police officers followed Pop into the living room.

'We'd also like to speak with your wife Sarah, and your daughter Katherine, if possible, sir.'

My eyes widened. 'They do know about us, Grandma, what are we going to do?'

Pop spoke. 'Oh, well, just hang on, Sarah is in the kitchen, and Katherine is upstairs.'

Mom, who'd obviously been listening as well, went straight through.

'Mrs Sarah Briscoe?' asked Detective Chief Inspector Doune.

'Yes,' said Mom, very calmly, 'how can I help?'

'I'm afraid we're investigating the disappearance of Marcas Wilson. We believe your daughter and Marcas are at the same school and are good friends?'

I stared at Grandma, a look of horror on my face. I couldn't believe Marcas had disappeared.

'That's right, yes,' Mom answered. 'Maybe it's best if she joins us.'

Mom came to the foot of the stairs and looked up, but by that time I was already bounding downstairs.

'I overheard, Mom.' I turned to DCI Doune. 'This can't be true, can it? Marcas spent the day with us on Saturday and stayed overnight. Then we all went to Pets Corner on Sunday morning and I spoke to him on the phone later, when he'd gone home. He was fine then. Absolutely fine.'

'Yes, we do know there was a phone call between you and Marcas on Sunday, miss, and another one between Mrs Briscoe and Marcas shortly afterwards. We'd like to know what those conversations were about, if you'd be so kind?'

'Well,' I said, trying to get my thoughts straight, 'I phoned him because I'd had an unexpected present that we thought might have been a hoax sent by Marcas. He's full of pranks, you know.'

'And what did he say?'

'He just said he didn't send it, that it was against his principles to send presents. He's like me, you see, he doesn't like the fact that everyone buys so much stuff that they don't really need. It uses up Earth's resources.'

'And that's all?'

'Yes. I mean, no. We arranged to meet at Pets Corner, by The Hooligoats. He's good at technical things and I couldn't work out how to use the ARK, so he said he could help.'

'The ARK miss? That was the present that you thought was a hoax?'

Out of the corner of my eye, I could see Mom stiffen. 'It was, yes.'

'And was it a hoax?'

'Er, no. No it wasn't.'

'So, may we see this… ARK present, miss?'

'Er, no, I don't have it anymore. It's gone. Is it important?'

'At this moment, miss, everything is important. What you are telling me is that you had a present that you thought was a hoax, but wasn't a hoax, and you don't have it anymore, even though you received it just a few days ago. Is that correct?'

'Yes.'

'Could you tell us where you were, please, on the morning of Sunday?'

'I've told you, we all went to Pets Corner. With Marcas.'

'Hmmm, yet you phoned him later that same day, to meet at Pets Corner again.' DCI Doune turned to Mom before I could answer. 'Mrs Briscoe, could you tell me what your conversation with Marcas was about, please?'

'I phoned to tell him that my daughter had changed her mind and he didn't need to go to Pets Corner.'

'And had she? Had she changed her mind?'

'I, er, I just thought that I would go along to meet her instead, so Marcas didn't need to.'

'So your daughter was still expecting Marcas to turn up?'

'Yes, I presume so.'

'And then you went along to Pets Corner?'

'Yes, I went about half an hour after my daughter.'

'Yes,' said the DCI, looking at her notebook, 'your daughter was observed entering Pets Corner at 14:05. You were observed entering at 14:40, and Mr Briscoe was also seen entering a little later at 14:45. According to our witness, Mr Briscoe was looking "furtive". We also understand that there were some strange screaming and howling noises emanating from the area at 14:15. Could you explain those, Miss Briscoe?'

I could feel myself blushing. I could hardly say there was a human-shaped koala bear called Gertie on the loose. 'No, I, er, didn't hear anything.'

'Hmmm. We're also told, although our witness is

unclear about timing, that you all re-emerged sometime later, but you sir,' she looked at Pop, 'you were in an unconscious state and being pushed along by your wife and daughter in a wheelbarrow. This all sounds somewhat bizarre to us, sir, but our witness is adamant. Could someone, anyone, enlighten us please?'

'It was all so embarrassing,' said Pop. 'I just felt very unwell, I think the fresh air must have got to me, and I had to be carried home. In the, erm, wheelbarrow. Completely innocent, I assure you.'

'Really? I do hope you're recovered now, sir. But, at this point, let me tell you all that Marcas Wilson left his parents' house just after the call from you ma'am. Told his parents that Mrs Briscoe had said to him not to bother going, but he was off to see the cat anyway?'

'Oh, that's me,' I interrupted. 'Kat, short for Katherine, and, er, Kathlene. My friends call me The Kat.'

'Ah, that explains that, thank you. Marcas was then observed entering Pets Corner shortly afterwards. That's the last anyone has seen of him. Unless you saw him, miss?'

How could that be?

'No, he didn't come round to me. I don't know where he can have got to.'

'Well, at the moment we're keeping an open mind, but let's just say that the behaviour of all three of you is more than a little odd. We may well need to speak with you further.'

I felt close to tears. 'Is anyone looking for him?' I asked.

'We've had teams out in his village, miss, after he was reported missing, and we're about to widen the operation.

We did a check of Pets Corner, especially where the pygmy goats are kept but we didn't get anything. Apart from the sergeant here, who got bruises on her shins where the larger goat headbutted her.'

'Trust Barney,' I muttered.

'Barney, miss?'

'Oh, he's the one with the big horns. We call him the Badass because he's a, erm… badass.'

'We'll keep that in mind, miss, thank you.'

Then Pop asked, 'Can you tell us who the witness is, Inspector?'

'It was actually a young lady who was out walking. I can't give you her name, I'm afraid, sir. All I can say is that she doesn't come from around here, but is visiting a relative. In fact, the young lady comes from a village right up in the north of Scotland. Place I haven't heard of but, then again, I'm not familiar with north-of-the-border. Now, if anyone remembers anything else, please call me. Here's my card.' She gave Pop a small business card and turned to leave.

Pop showed her out and came back into the living room, closely followed by Grandma. We all stared at each other.

Grandma was the first to speak. 'I think we need a cup of tea,' she said. 'Maybe a biscuit as well.'

'Bit early for biscuits, Grandma,' said Pop, 'it's only nine o'clock.'

'It's never too early for a biscuit, young man.'

Ten minutes later, the three of us were sitting down with mugs of tea, and Grandma had her packet of biscuits.

I felt more than a little anxious after being grilled by the police, so I blurted out, 'This is really awful. Poor Marcas. And his parents must be devastated. Do you think the police suspect us? I can't believe I told them about the ARK. What a dinklebrain I am.'

'Calm down, Kat, calm down,' said Grandma. 'Sentiment is fine so, yes, poor Marcas, but this calls for action. And don't worry about mentioning the ARK. The ARK can look after itself.'

'What do you suggest, Grandma?' I asked.

'Well, what we know is that Marcas has disappeared, and that a young Scottish woman appears to have witnessed your movements on Sunday.'

I blushed again. 'Oh, you know about the pooping. Sorry, I couldn't help it.'

'NOT bowel movements, Kat. I meant your movements into, and out of, Pets Corner.'

'Oh, sorry, I understand.'

'As I was saying, we also know that Marcas was not seen at Pets Corner by any of you three or, indeed, by Gertie. What we don't know is what happened to him. And how did that young lady manage to see what you were all doing, without being spotted herself?'

Grandma sat quietly, contemplating.

'Grandma?' Mom said.

'Just thinking. We obviously need to find out where Marcas is, before the police start poking around in Huldufólk business. So we need to ask questions. Reginald, you chat with Mr Brown and Mr Gohturd. They're as good at gossiping as anyone. Mom, you talk with Bossy Barbara, she thinks she owns everything and everybody, so she may have heard or seen something odd. Kat, you go talk with The Hooligoats, they usually know more than they let on.'

'And what will you do, Grandma?' I asked.

'I'm going to take a look from upstairs.'

'You can't see much from the bedroom windows,' Pop said, clearly as puzzled as I was.

'By upstairs, I mean skywards. I'm going chiropteran.'

We all looked blank.

'As a bat,' Grandma explained impatiently. 'I'm going to transmogrify into my bat form straight away, and take an aerial view.'

'Oh,' said Pop. 'Straight away? But what about breakfast?'

'Have a biscuit,' replied Grandma.

—

Luckily, there was a break in the weather. It had stopped raining, and the wind had died down. The forecasters were saying another storm front was moving in, though, so we wouldn't have much time before needing to head home.

As I headed out to Pets Corner, I spotted Grandma wheeling about in the sky overhead. Bats look very odd, I've always thought, when they're flying. They don't keep in a straight line, but have a somewhat erratic path, appearing to dodge one way, then another. Grandma was no exception. Sometimes I thought she would crash into the telegraph poles that lined the road, but she always veered off at the last moment. A couple of red kites kept well away from where she was flying. I wasn't sure whether they felt threatened by the fact that she was a vampire bat, or by her unpredictable flying technique.

When I got to The Hooligoats, they were all lined up motionless against the fence, staring out in the direction of the lane.

'Er, hello lads. Is everything okay?'

They didn't move, or bleat. It was as though they were in a trance.

'I'm going to change into my goat form,' I said, a little nervously.

No response.

'Okay, ready or not, here I come.'

This would be my first solo attempt. I focused on Ralph, then closed my eyes and concentrated all of my mind on changing. After a few seconds, I felt myself getting smaller and smaller. I opened my eyes and trotted over to Cuthbert.

'Have I changed properly?' I asked.

'Sssh,' he whispered.

'Is my head changed? I worry about my head.'

'SHUSH,' demanded Barney.

'We're listening,' explained Ralph in a whisper.

'To what?'

In the distance there was a faint clip-clopping.

'HORSE!' shouted Fernando.

The Hooligoats turned and headed for the shed.

Ralph looked back at me as they went. 'Come on, Kat, or you'll miss it.'

I had no idea what was going on, but curiosity got the better of me again. Once inside the shed, Barney went over to the back wall and pushed at one of the vertical planks of wood, which obligingly slid to one side, revealing a small pathway into the car park. One by one, the lads piled through, closely followed by me. Then we all broke into a run and headed towards the lane.

'I didn't realise there was an opening at the back of the shed,' I said, breathlessly.

Barney answered, 'Course there is. How do you think we get out to go to the café?'

Incredulous, I asked, 'You all go to the café?'

'Oh yes. Only at night, though. We can't afford the daytime prices.'

'But it's only open during the day,' I said.

'That's why it's cheaper at night then. Stands to reason.' Barney turned his head and winked at me. 'It's also why we installed a secret door in the café storeroom.'

'But how did… Oh, never mind.'

As we emerged into the lane, the horse and its rider were just going past. They cantered along the road and disappeared round the corner.

'Curses,' muttered Barney. 'Nothing happened. Maybe next time.' He turned, and we all started walking back towards the shed.

'So,' I said, starting to feel irritated at the fact that we'd run all the way out here, only to be going back again. 'What exactly were you expecting to happen?'

'We were hoping that the horse would pee, and that Bossy Barbara would come out and sit in it.'

My irritation started to boil over. 'And just why ON EARTH would she do that?' I demanded.

'Ralph overheard her talking to Mr Gohturd,' Barney said.

Fernando giggled.

'She said she would have to go into horse piddle.'

I stopped, and looked intently at Barney. 'Give me strength,' I muttered. 'Are you serious? Or is this just a joke?'

Barney stared back. 'What do you mean?' he asked indignantly.

'Well, I have a feeling, just a feeling, mind, that Bossy Barbara might have said she was going into hospital, not into horse piddle. She just has a plummy way of talking.'

'Oh,' said Barney.

'How very disappointing,' sighed Ralph.

–

As we walked back to the shed, I explained to them about Marcas going missing, and about the last sighting of him being at Pets Corner.

'That's really bad news,' said Ralph. 'He certainly didn't come round by our pen, or we'd have seen him. Which means that something must have happened to him beforehand, maybe by where the birdcages are.'

'Good thinking,' I said. 'How do we find out?'

'Leave it to us, we'll pop out again after dark and ask all the other animals. Now, Mr Gohturd is due to come and feed us, so you need to get out of here.'

'Thank you. Thank you. But guys?'

'Yes?'

'Be careful. Grandma says that something bad is coming.'

Ralph nodded. 'We know. Mother Earth is throwing a bit of a wobbly.'

'You know about that stuff, about listening to Mother Earth?'

Cuthbert looked puzzled. 'Course we do. Don't you?'

'No, Grandma says I will learn to, but she didn't say when.'

Cuthbert looked at Ralph, and I'm sure he winked. 'No worries,' he said encouragingly. 'We can show you. Just lie down on your side with your ear on the ground.'

I did as he suggested, but got up again a few moments later.

'I don't know,' I said, undecided about whether I'd connected with Mother Earth. 'All I got was a tickling sensation in my nostril.'

Ralph and Cuthbert burst into laughter. 'That's not how you do it,' spluttered Cuthbert. 'We just wondered whether that spider would crawl up your nose. Ha ha ha ha ha.'

Eughhh.

As the two of them wandered off, I sneezed. A slightly soggy spider landed on the ground in front of me, shook itself, and made a dash for the cover of a fence post.

–

Mom, Pop, Grandma and I sat down that evening to tell each other about any progress we'd made in finding out what had happened to Marcas. Before we got to the main business, I told them about the horse piddle incident. I think we were all really stressed about Marcas, so it was a welcome break in the tension, and everyone laughed loudly. Unfortunately, the respite didn't last long.

The doorbell rang, and this time Mom opened the door.

'Oh, hello again, Inspector.'

As soon as I heard Mom say the word "Inspector" I rushed to find out what was happening.

'Have you found him?' I asked breathlessly. 'Have you found Marcas?'

'I'm afraid not, miss,' replied DCI Doune. 'This is a different matter. We're here to talk to you all about the brutal murder of your neighbour, Mr Brown. What's left of him was found by his son just a short while ago. Whoever did it clearly wanted us to believe it was an animal attack.'

Chapter Ten

Into Thin Air

—

When she'd heard DCI Doune talking about an animal attack, there was no holding Grandma back. She came racing to the front door much faster than I would have thought possible.

'Did I hear you mention that you thought it might be an animal attack? It just so happens that I've been a consultant for Dudley Zoo on animal behaviour. May I come and see?'

I looked at Mom, who shrugged and shook her head almost imperceptibly.

The Inspector was not to be easily persuaded. 'And you are?' she asked.

'I'm Grandma.'

'I mean what is your name?'

'I told you, Grandma. Just Grandma will do fine.'

Inspector Doune had obviously come across people before who preferred not to identify themselves.

'I see,' she said. 'Well, Just Grandma, I'm afraid that until I can establish your credentials, Mr Brown's house is a crime scene that is off-limits. To everyone.' She stepped

inside the front door and started to make her way through
to the living room. 'Now, there are a number of questions
I'd like to ask you all.'

–

I don't think for a moment that DCI Doune suspected
any of us of killing Mr Brown. After all, she was totally
unaware that both Mom and Grandma could shape-shift
into animals that could 'tear someone's throat out'. It was
about an hour later, however, before she decided she had
enough detail and could leave us in peace. Not that there
could be much peace when Marcas had disappeared and
Mr Brown had been horribly murdered.

But Grandma was not to be deterred by his house
being declared a crime scene. She announced she was
going to have a peek inside.

Pop tried to stop her. 'But Grandma, you can't get in.
The police have sealed it off.'

'They've sealed it off so that people can't get in, I doubt
whether they've sealed it off against a determined bat.'

There was a flutter of wings, and Grandma was on her
way.

–

'So, do you think it was an animal attack?'

It was half an hour later, and Grandma had just got
back from Mr Brown's house. I was desperate to know
what she thought.

'It certainly looks like it, and a fairly vicious kind of animal it must have been,' she said, pensively. 'Some of the cushions on the settee had been torn to shreds, and there were deep scratch marks on two of the inside doors. Trouble is...'

Pop was just as impatient as me. 'Trouble is what, Grandma?'

'Trouble is, there is no sign of forced entry. Nothing at all to suggest a break-in. Which, in turn, suggests that Mr Brown knew his attacker.'

'And he wouldn't let a wild animal into his house like that, would he?' I asked. 'I mean, could the police be right when they say it was a person who killed him, and made it look like an animal attack?'

'Yes,' replied Grandma, still obviously perplexed by the situation. 'That's the best explanation, I think. I just don't like the fact that Marcas' disappearance is followed so closely by this killing. I can't help but wonder whether they're connected.'

That was the first time I felt panic starting to bubble away inside me. 'Do you mean that Marcas may be lying dead somewhere? That someone has killed him as well?'

'I think what we need to do is to sit down calmly and go through what we've found out so far. Tea and biscuits would help. Reginald.'

–

In fact, none of us had turned up anything useful. It was devastating. Mr Gohturd and Bronwen, who live in the same village as Marcas, had seen lots of police on the Monday, and had joined a search to check sheds, outhouses and barns in the area. But they hadn't seen anything suspicious on Sunday itself.

Pop had also talked to Mr Brown, obviously before Mr Brown had been murdered, who said he'd seen nothing unusual, but thought maybe he should head up a Neighbourhood Watch group.

Bossy Barbara hadn't seen anything personally, but her niece turned out to be the witness that had told the police about our movements (not the pooping variety) on the day in question. It turned out that BB, who's family originally comes from somewhere near Edinburgh, didn't even know she had a niece until Ailsa got in touch by phone the day before turning up. In fact, Bossy didn't want her niece to overhear the conversation with Mom, but apparently Ailsa is not particularly clean, has disgusting eating habits, and doesn't help around the house or Pets Corner. Worse than that, said Bossy, she sometimes slips out of the house when it's dark, and doesn't get back for hours. The most heinous crime, though, was that she used a knife to spread butter on her toast, then stuck it straight back in the butter. Complete with crumbs.

'Just what would the Ladies of the Village make of that?' Bossy had asked.

Mom had said that, if she had a niece like that, she wouldn't tolerate that kind of behaviour, but Bossy just replied by saying, 'Well, she's family.'

Grandma did lots of flights around the area, but spotted nothing out of the ordinary. And, if Ailsa was sneaking out at night, Grandma didn't spot her. She did report, however, that a couple of red kites had moved on to a different area.

In the meantime, the police were frequently seen in the village. Mr Brown's cottage was visited several times by Scene of Crime Officers, and the local canals and ponds were checked by police divers. Various appeals for information were made on local TV news and in the county newspapers.

Despite all of the activity, however, it was as though Marcas, and Mr Brown's murderer, had just disappeared into thin air without a trace.

—

As the days passed, the police made no progress, and their initial frenetic activity slowed significantly, though they did occasionally drive through the village. There were still plenty of social media posts about Marcas, however, usually saying that the reasons behind his disappearance were being covered up by police, and by his parents. People can be so horrible at times. Some even reckoned that he'd been spotted in France and Spain, which was such nonsense. He was close by, I just knew it.

Back at home, apart from the worries about Marcas, Grandma became increasingly concerned with the fact that the police and media attention, and the appalling weather, was preventing me from getting more practice in transmogrification. It was almost as though she thought there was a deadline that we had to work to. In a way, I suppose, she wanted me to be goat-perfect by the time of my Coming Out party, which I personally wasn't really bothered about. It seemed to me that Marcas' welfare was more important than meeting the real Kathlene, the one who could transmogrify into a gryphon. Not that I was in any way envious. Honestly.

As it happened, I managed to spend time *with* The Hooligoats, and even some time *as* a Hooligoat, so, when the day of the party arrived, I was as good at changing my form, from girl to goat and back again, as I thought I could be. And, more to the point, the lads hadn't played any more tricks on me. Quite the reverse, in fact, as they did their best to cheer me up, even to the extent of teaching me play-headbutting.

I have to admit, this was great fun, even better than I'd thought it would be after watching the goats doing it. It didn't make me forget about Marcas, he was always there in the thoughts at the back of my mind, but it did help me to see that I couldn't spend my days moping around.

Play-headbutting, if you didn't know, is when two goats face up to each other, rise up on back legs, then drop down and clash heads and horns. When they do this, it's playing. At least, that's what Barney told me. If one goat headbutts another one in the side, or the rear, then it's aggressive, maybe even bullying. At least, that's what Ralph told me. So, learning play-headbutting was fun, even if I got a headache after the first few times. And Cuthbert made me laugh every time when he was showing me how to do it. He didn't seem able to judge position very well, so when he got up onto his hind legs, he'd dance around as though he was doing a jig, then drop down and miss me completely. On one occasion, he pirouetted so much that he fell over backwards and knocked over a water bowl, and it splashed all over his head. We all howled with laughter when he got up, spluttering and shaking himself.

Chapter Eleven

Why ROAR When You Can Squeak?

O n the morning of the party itself came the news from The Elders that they thought we should limit the number of Familiars to just one, because more than that: 'would unnecessarily stretch one's ability to maintain proper control of the Familiar(s) in the event of any problems arising from a given situation'. I thought this was silly, and said so to Grandma.

She told me, 'Just remember that you haven't turned even one Familiar as yet, so you don't know what's involved. The Elders have experience in these things.'

'So what did you vote, Grandma?' I must say, I think I sounded a little petulant when I said that.

'What I voted is not of your concern, Kat, so please don't ask that question again. Now, go and get ready for the party. This is important to you, and you need to be paying close attention to proceedings.'

Probably because I was feeling a little aggrieved, I

remember wondering what did Grandma actually mean by that? *You need to be paying close attention to proceedings?* As you might have guessed, I was soon to find out…

–

I don't know what prompted it, but it was when the guests were starting to arrive that I suddenly got very morbid about Marcas, and I began to question my strongly held conviction that he was still alive. One thought led to another and, before I knew it, I started to panic about Pop as well. I couldn't let it rest.

'Mom, what happens to Pop?' I asked.

'Pop, dear? Well, he's not allowed to attend your Coming Out, I'm afraid, it's strictly a girls-only party. Your father will be working in the shed until your guests have all gone. The Elders think that having a human, especially a human male, would unsettle everyone to the point where they may not be able to demonstrate transmogrifying.'

'I didn't mean that, Mom. What I want to know is what happens to Pop when…' I began to choke on the words, 'when he gets old.'

'Ah, I think I see where you're going, dear. Should we have a chat about it afterwards?'

'No, it's in my head, I can't think of anything else. Grandma says that she is as old as she wants to be. So if she can be old one minute, and then young again, that must mean that Huldufólk live a long time. Longer than humans?'

'Well, just to be clear, we can only go backwards in age. A Huldufólk woman who has not been any older than twenty couldn't suddenly become sixty years old. That wouldn't be possible. But someone who is twenty years old could become, say, fifteen again. And someone who is sixty years old can go back to being twenty years old, or fifty-nine if she so wishes.'

'So how long do we live?' I demanded.

'I don't think I know, Kat. As far as I'm aware, no Huldufólk woman has ever died of natural causes.'

'And Pop? Now that he knows about Huldufólk, will he live forever too?'

'I'm afraid knowing about us won't make any difference to how long your father lives. When a husband grows old, he will eventually die. There is nothing we can do about that. Not even our magic can change the fact that your father won't be around forever. And, in that respect, you are no different from a human child.'

'I hate that.'

'I know, dear. I hate it too. But we just have to get used to it. It's a fact of life, both Huldufólk and human. And also, unfortunately, a fact of death.'

Tears started streaming down my face. 'What will you do when Pop dies?'

'I don't know. I don't think we ever know until we get to a situation like that. Some Huldufólk ladies choose to become a younger age and find someone else to love. Others, like your grandma, don't feel that the person they once loved can be replaced.'

I hugged Mom tightly, still crying. 'There's no-one that can replace Pop.'

'I know, dear, I know. But your pop is still a young man.

Well, youngish. It'll be some time before we have to decide. And I'll make sure to involve you in whatever happens.'

She lifted my face and dried my tears away.

'Now, your guests are waiting. It's time to strut your stuff.'

–

Strutting my stuff is a term that makes me cringe. It makes me sound like a performing seal. Not that I have anything against seals, you understand. Some Huldufólk can actually shape-shift into seals, and some into penguins. One that I know can turn into a duck-billed platypus, though that's a different story. But I knew what Mom meant, so I dried my eyes, put on my best smile, and went through to the other room, where there was instant applause and cheering.

The first one to give me a hug, though, was Kathlene. I'm not sure what it was about her, but she didn't look like an I-can-shape-shift-into-a-gryphon kind of girl. There's nothing wrong with that, of course. It's just that, when you look at someone, it can be quite fun to try to work out what animal they would suit. And I couldn't picture Kathlene as a gryphon.

Anyway, she hugged me so tightly that I could hardly breathe, and then she whispered in my ear, 'I need to speak with you. Meet me in the garden in five minutes.'

What on earth was going on, I wondered? After hugs with everyone else, I made my excuses and slipped out through the back door, and into the garden. Kathlene was sitting on the swing. I went over to her.

'What's wrong? You didn't sound very happy.'

'Oh, I really am happy, thank you,' said Kathlene. 'Mother just said I shouldn't let it come as a surprise to you.' She smiled gently at me, as if trying to prepare me for what she was about to say.

'Let what be a surprise?'

'That I can't turn into a gryphon.'

I was NOT expecting that, so avoiding a surprise had failed at the first hurdle. 'You can't…' I said in amazement.

'… turn into a gryphon,' she said, completing my sentence for me.

'But, I don't understand. Grandma and Mom told me that your chosen animal at our baptism was a gryphon. How can you not be able to become one? Didn't the ARK help you?'

'Not really, no,' Kathlene replied.

'Look, maybe you'd better tell me what happened. From the beginning.'

I sat on the swing next to Kathlene. She looked at her hands, which were clasped together on her lap, and started to explain.

'Well, you know that there was a mix-up, and I was supposed to be able to become this half-lion, half-eagle thing?'

'A gryphon, yes.'

'When it came to it, I just didn't believe that I could do it. Or even that I wanted to. Mother showed me pictures of one and, I have to say, they were fairly fearsome-looking creatures. Not my kind of thing at all. And, more importantly, there are no gryphons around now. That's if there ever were any in the first place. Mother thinks they were only mythological, that they never actually existed. So, the ARK seemed to sense my feelings, and it gave up and disappeared.'

'Oh. And?'

'Well, how did you first change into a pygmy goat without the aid of the ARK?'

'I stared hard at one of them. Concentrated in my mind.'

'And I couldn't do that, because I didn't have one to stare at.'

'So what did you do?'

'As I said, Mother showed me a picture of one in a book. *Myths, Folklore and Legends* it was called. I concentrated hard on the picture for ages. Eventually, I transmogrified.'

'Into a gryphon?'

'No, silly, into a book. I turned into a copy of *Myths, Folklore and Legends*. That felt weird, I can tell you. I had thousands and thousands of words, and dozens of pictures and illustrations in my head all at the same time.'

I was dumbstruck at the thought, and I had to work hard to resist the temptation to laugh out loud. I'd never even considered the possibility that a Huldufólk could turn into an inanimate object. Having said that, though, books are made from paper, which in turn is made from the wood from trees, so books are made from something that *used* to be alive.

'Anyway,' she continued, 'Mother gave me a hug, and I changed back to me. Though I still have nightmares about being chased around by random numbers and letters. Fortunately, Mother and I went to see The Elders and, because of the mix-up at the baptism, they agreed to break with tradition and allow me to be re-baptised and assigned a different animal.'

I hardly dared ask. But I did. 'Well... what *do* you change into, then?'

It took me several minutes to let the answer sink in.

'Oh,' said Kathlene, 'I'm a lovely, sweet little gerbil. I'll show you later.'

Chapter Twelve

To Be, or Not To Be

———

As soon as I got back into the house, I found Mom, who was busy slicing cake in the kitchen, and pushed her into the hallway.

'Mom, did you know about this?' I demanded.

'Know about what, dear?'

'About Kathlene not being able to transform into a gryphon.'

'Surely that's not possible. She was baptised —'

'And she was re-baptised. So that she could become a gerbil.'

Mom genuinely seemed as surprised as I was. 'A what, dear?'

'A gerbil,' I repeated.

'A gerbil? Not a gryphon?'

I couldn't help mimicking Kathlene. 'A lovely, sweet little gerbil.'

'But… no I didn't know. Let's find Grandma.'

We hunted round, and eventually found Grandma upstairs, lying down on her bed. As Mom and I entered, she raised herself up on her elbows.

'Ah,' she said, smiling, 'so, Kat, were you paying close attention, then? What do you think?'

'What I think, Grandma, is that Kathlene was re-baptised so that she could become a sweet little gerbil, and you were one of The Elders who allowed her to do that. And you have never told me that I could be re-baptised so that I could become a gryphon.'

'Well,' said Grandma, calmly, 'Kathlene was allowed to be re-baptised because she couldn't become a gryphon, and it would never have suited her. She's a fairly timid child.'

'And me? Why couldn't I be re-baptised?'

'Because you were able to become a goat, so there was no need. Don't you like changing into a goat? Becoming one of The Hooligoats?'

'Well... yes, of course I do. But that's not the point, Grandma.'

'What *is* the point, then?'

I stamped my foot. 'The point is... the point is...' And then it dawned on me. 'The point is, Grandma, that Kathlene changed into something that wasn't defined at her baptism. She should never have been able to become a book.'

Grandma smiled broadly. 'So you *were* paying close attention, well done. And you are quite right. We reckon that Kathlene is what Dr Steiner refers to as an Aberrant. She seems to have a slight glitch in the genetic code that Frankie used when she developed our line of Huldufólk.'

'So,' I insisted, 'if she's changed once into something that she shouldn't have been able to, could she do it again? Could she become something other than a gerbil?'

'Highly unlikely, we think. The only danger is that she bites someone. Gerbils have teeth like needles, you know.'

'But it could happen?'

'Technically? Yes, it could.'

'But that's so unfair. I wish I could change into whatever I wanted.'

'Ah, but it is what it is, Kat. Some things were just meant to be. And we'll be keeping an eye on her. She lives in Netherton, a few streets away from Ma Pardoe's, and one of The Elders lives nearby. If she changes into anything else, we'll know about it.'

–

By the time we got to the Coming Out Parade, I still wasn't in any mood to take part. It was all so very confusing. Grandma was right, of course, I really, really enjoyed being able to transmogrify into a Hooligoat. They were my favourite animals in the whole wide world, even if they got spiders to crawl up my nose. But I couldn't help feeling that to be a gryphon would be so... so totally awesome. If I'd been a gryphon, maybe I'd have been able to find Marcas.

Mom kept hold of my hand, squeezing it every now and again.

'Kat, I want you to know that I love you,' she said. 'And, whether you're a pygmy goat or a gryphon, I'm incredibly proud of you. As is your father, of course. I, we, both want you to be happy.' She kissed the top of my head. 'Please be happy?' I couldn't help it. I smiled back. Mom had a way of making things feel right again.

So, the parade got underway. Apparently it was the first of its kind for several years.

Now, what can I say about the parade? I know the intention was to get all the Huldufólk offspring to change to their respective animal-form and stand, or perch, in a line with us newbies at the front, ready for a photoshoot. So, I had it in mind that it would be a civilised and orderly procession of well-groomed Huldufólk transmogrifications.

No chance.

Even new-born puppies can be taught bite-inhibition quite quickly, but it seems that teenage Huldufólk who turn into carnivorous critters are not so easily disciplined, and do their best to maintain their place in the food-chain. So, a somewhat dishevelled Veronica the vixen raced around trying to take a chunk out of Jenny the bedraggled chicken, whilst Tina the balding owl took flight and circled round the room, greedily eying up Rachel the tail-less mouse, who was desperately trying to hide under the sideboard.

It took about half an hour for the adults to re-establish calm. All the teens were thoroughly scolded, and instructed to resume human form, which they did, reluctantly. Poor Jemima the confused Siamese cat stroke dachshund, however, had to be taken to the vet to see if they could re-attach her ear after she'd been attacked by Angie the flatulent ferret. Still, at least I got to find out that there's such a thing as a Huldufólk vet. Never know when that may come in useful...

At the end of it all, when all was settled again, it was time for Kathlene and me to demonstrate to everyone what we could do. Having seen the chaos created by the others, we were much more comfortable with showing off our skills.

And, much as I hate to admit it, that gerbil was soooo adorable.

~

When our guests had gone, Pop was allowed back into the house.

'Just as well,' he said, 'my feet were beginning to freeze out there in the shed.'

'Didn't you put the heater on, dear?' asked Mom.

'There's a heater in there?'

Pop was never very observant. Just like me, really.

'Oh, well,' he said, turning to me. 'How did your party go? Did I miss much?'

'It was appalling, Pop. There was a really cute gerbil, a cat stroke doggie that lost an ear, and the rest were all trying to eat each other. Nothing as exotic as a gryphon, mind you. In fact, did you know, Pop, that Kathlene doesn't turn into a gryphon? Hard to believe, I know, but no-one does. Especially me. I'm a goat.'

'Oh...' Pop didn't seem to know what to say, so I carried on regardless.

'Grandma says that some things were just meant to be. What do you think about that, Pop?'

'Er, am I going to get into any trouble if I tell you that what Grandma says sounds sensible?'

I suddenly realised that I was being stupid. 'No, of

course not, Pop. Sorry. Much as I love being able to be a Hooligoat, I just have this feeling, deep inside, that I should have been something truly awesome.'

'But the goats ARE awesome, Kat, and we love 'em to bits, don't we? Tell you what, let's go round and see them now. I've got plenty of fifty-pence pieces. It'll be dark in a couple of hours, but we still have time, and it always cheers you up.'

'Okay, but there's another storm blowing in, Pop, we'll have to hurry.'

–

As Pop and I were walking the short distance to Pets Corner, we were so busy talking that neither of us realised that something was suddenly directly in front of us until I strode straight into it. It felt as though I'd walked into a tree, and I thought I must have been dazed and not seeing things clearly, because whatever it was seemed to take a few seconds to rearrange itself into the figure of a woman.

She stood facing us, her gaze fixed firmly on Pop. She smiled.

'I'm so sorry,' she said in a very gentle Scottish accent, 'I didn't see you there. My fault.'

'Er, hello,' said Pop. 'No, we were too wrapped up in conversation so our fault, I think. I, er, I haven't seen you around before.'

The girl smiled again. 'I'm Ailsa. I only drifted in a short time ago. Here visiting an aunt and, kind of, checking out the area. But you must be Reginald. I've heard so much about you.'

It was obvious that Pop took an instant liking to her. It was also obvious that she was intent on ignoring me completely. I wasn't going to be put off so easily, though.

'Hello, Ailsa,' I said, 'your name is a really old Celtic one, isn't it? Oddly enough, I had a friend at school with the same name. It means *Supernatural Victory*, if I remember correctly.'

She looked at me with eyes that seemed to pierce mine.

'Hmmm,' she muttered, 'I see you.'

What an odd thing to say, I thought to myself, *of course she can see me, she's looking straight at me.*

'Pop,' I said, 'shall we go see The Hooligoats? Mr Gohturd must be about to put them to bed for the night. That's if you can tear yourself away from Ailsa…'

Pop seemed very reluctant. 'Er yes, why not?' he said, his eyes still firmly fixed on the face of his new-found friend.

I grabbed his arm and steered him away, almost pushing him round the corner to The Hooligoats' shed. Sure enough, we were just in time to find Mr Gohturd putting out the last feed of the day. He'd developed a feeding routine that was always hilarious to watch, especially now, as the lads were oblivious to our presence. All they were interested in was how much of their own, and everybody else's food they could eat.

Firstly, Mr Gohturd placed the four empty bowls on a small table, and got the sack of feed and a small jug, which he used to measure an equal amount into each bowl.

While he was doing this, the goats, excepting Barney who stood patiently by the entrance to the shed, paced around and tried to stand up at the table to see whether they could sneak a nibble from the bowls. Mr Gohturd kept nudging the bowls out of reach, though, so the lads couldn't quite get to them. Once the bowls were ready, Mr Gohturd took one of them and went inside the shed, with Barney following close behind. Barney had to be fed separately from the others because he used to push the other three out of the way so that he could eat all the food.

Unfortunately, when Mr Gohturd went inside the shed, the other three bowls were left unattended and Cuthbert stood up against the table, stretched his neck as much as he could, and grabbed one of the bowls in his mouth. There was a clatter as the bowl fell to the ground and the three Hooligoats once again lived up to their name, as they scrabbled to eat the food that had fallen on the floor. Mr Gohturd came racing out of the shed and bent down to pick up the bowl, which was now empty. While he was bending over, Barney sneaked back out of the shed and gently headbutted his behind, and he fell flat on the grass, muttering to himself.

After picking himself up, Mr Gohturd pushed Barney back into the shed and closed the door so that he couldn't get back out, then re-filled the empty bowl and placed all three on the ground, firstly for Fernando, then quickly for Ralph, and finally for Cuthbert. As usual, Ralph and Fernando finished before Cuthbert, so they tried hard to push him out of the way. All three of them ended up dancing round each other, standing on hind legs, doing play-headbutting, kicking food bowls around, and generally making a mess.

After all this chaos, Mr Gohturd cleared away, washed the bowls, and settled all the goats into the shed for the night, firmly closing and bolting the door so that they couldn't get out. Of course, he was blissfully unaware of the fact that the lads had a secret exit at the rear of the shed.

Having spent about half an hour watching this, I told Mr Gohturd that we were going back home and as we turned, I motioned for Pop to carry on without me and quietly made my way round the back of the shed to where the moveable plank was. I knocked gently on the wood and, after a few moments, it slid to one side and Ralph peered out. I had to transform into my goat form before I could get through the gap.

'Hello,' Ralph said, 'you're here late.'

'I know,' I replied. 'I just wanted to talk to you about Marcas. Have you heard anything yet? He's been gone a long time now and I'm beyond worried.'

'Nothing,' said Ralph. 'We've asked around quite a few times, especially out in the fields, but none of the other animals has heard, or seen, anything of Marcas. Don't worry, I'm sure he'll turn up.'

Barney came over.

'Did you see me get Gohturd?' he asked. 'I couldn't resist the invitation. You could call it butting his butt. I bet he won't do that again in a hurry.'

Ralph could see how concerned I was. 'Look, we'll go out again later, ask around again. See if anyone knows anything.'

'Okay,' I said quietly. 'Please try to find him, I have this feeling something awful has happened to him.'

–

After resuming my human form, I started back towards the lane, only to find Pop chatting away again to Ailsa.

'Time to get back, Pop,' I called.

'Ah, must go,' Pop said to Ailsa. 'Lovely to have met you.'

Ailsa smiled in a way that gave me the creeps. 'Yes, I have to go too. Places to go, people to eat. Sorry, I meant… people to meet.'

Believe it or not, but Pop actually did a little bow to Ailsa. I thought I might do a curtsy, just out of devilment. But I didn't.

–

Back at home, dinner was about to be dished up.

'Met that Ailsa lady,' Pop said, almost dreamily I thought. 'Very pleasant she is. Strange eyes, but very, very pleasant.'

'Hmmm, Mom, better watch out. Pop has got a new friend.'

Pop blushed.

I couldn't resist adding, 'She's very odd though, she jokes about eating people and smirks in a way that reminds me of that poem about the smile of a crocodile.'

After that, dinner was eaten without very much conversation at all. At the end of it came the usual comment about washing up, and me being the dishwasher. I couldn't summon the willpower to argue the point, so I began to carry things through to the kitchen.

Pop called through to me, 'Give me a shout when you're ready, and I'll come through to dry the crocks.'

'Okay, will do.'

Washing up wasn't that bad really. It gave me time to think. Not always about anything in particular, I suppose, I just let my thoughts wander. On that day, though, I remember I was thinking about a news report that said that increased internet streaming and social media usage, together with faster technology, required more and more computer servers. This meant that there were thousands and thousands of hosting computers around the world, many of which were using dirty energy and this, in turn, had a polluting effect on the environment. It seemed, I thought, that Grandma was right. Mother Earth was being affected in ways we didn't really think about. Things that we took for granted were actually damaging the environment.

It didn't take long before I was ready for Pop to come through to start drying. I took my rubber gloves off and turned to go back through to the living room. As I did so, the outside lights in the garden came on and I could see someone standing outside, peering through the kitchen window. It was Ailsa. She was close enough to the house to have triggered the lighting, and I could see her quite clearly. As I stared at her, she stared straight back into my eyes and scowled. Her eyes glowed red, and she turned and headed off over the lawn.

I ran to the back door, but by the time I'd unlocked it and stepped outside she'd gone, and all I could see was the tail of a large dog as it disappeared through the garden gate, which was left swinging to and fro in the wind.

I quickly raced back into the house, and through to the living room. 'Pop,' I shouted, breathlessly. 'Ailsa was just in our garden. She scowled and ran off when she looked at me.'

'Really?' said Pop with a look of surprise. 'How did she…'

Grandma was quicker off the mark.

'Ailsa?' she demanded. 'Bossy Barbara's niece? The one from Scotland?' She squeezed past me and into the kitchen.

'She was looking through the window,' I said, following her. 'And it may have been nothing more than the reflection of the lights, but her eyes seemed to glow red when I turned and saw her. That was when she ran off. And I think there was a big dog with her. I saw its tail as it went through the gate.'

Grandma's eyes widened and she stood open-mouthed for a while. Once she'd regained her composure, she hurried outside, looking all around as she went. Then she lifted her head up and started sniffing the air. Round the garden she went, all the time sniffing, until she got to the garden gate. Mom and Pop had come out and were standing by me. Grandma stopped sniffing and stood, a look of puzzlement on her face.

'How odd,' she said, more to herself than to us, 'but that smell reminds me of something. Just can't remember what.'

Grandma seemed to be undecided for a few moments, before speaking again.

'Damn. Right, well, just to be on the safe side, everyone. Back inside please. I need to make a phone call.'

'What's the matter, Grandma? Ailsa seemed such a lovely young lady,' Pop wanted to know, as Grandma ushered us all into the house and locked the back door behind us.

Grandma sounded worried. 'I'm not sure Ailsa is who she appears to be, young man. In fact, I'm not even convinced that she is *what* she appears to be.' She nudged us into the living room and closed the door before going along the hallway to the telephone. There was what sounded like a very tense conversation, then Grandma came back into the living room.

'I have to go meet with the other Elders. I'll fly there tonight and be back as soon as I can.'

Mom interrupted, 'But Grandma, you can't possibly fly in this weather, it's far too windy.'

Grandma hesitated and thought. Then she said, 'Well, that can't be helped. I have to go, whatever the weather is doing. It's not that far to Dudley.'

'How about if we go by car? I'll drive you,' suggested Mom.

Grandma thought again. 'No, on second thoughts, I think we should all stay here tonight while it's dark, so that I can hang guard. In the morning, when it's light, you can take me in the car, Sarah.'

'Er, are we in danger from that girl?' asked Pop, anxiously.

'Look, I don't know for certain what we're dealing with, so we need to take whatever precautions we can. Firstly, we keep all external doors closed and locked unless you're actually going through them. In fact, don't go through them, stay inside the house. Same with windows. Secondly, Sarah and I will set off as soon as it's light and Kat and Pop then need to go and check on The Hooligoats. And whatever you do, Kat, do not try to turn them into Familiars. I know what you're like when your curiosity is roused.'

'Grandma?' I whispered.

'Yes, Kat?'

'I have a bad feeling about this. Do you think it's because I'm managing to connect with Mother Earth?'

'I've told you, Kat. When you connect with Mother Earth, you'll know about it. We all will.'

She smiled. 'Time to lock up, I think. We have a busy day ahead of us tomorrow.'

When she said that, I don't think she realised just how right she would turn out to be.

Chapter Thirteen
Pop Does Hoolispeak

———

That night was an uncomfortable one. I could hear Mom and Pop talking about things, both of them sounding really worried. And at some point during the night I got out of bed to go for a pee. I know I should have been expecting it, but I was still quite startled when I almost bumped into a large bat hanging upside down from the ceiling light on the landing.

The wind still gusted violently, and I could hear things clattering around outside as they were blown about. At least, I hoped it was just the wind that was blowing things around. The thought that Ailsa might be outside, whatever she might be, was not a pleasant one.

After what seemed like an endless night, came the dawn. I suppose it was inevitable that I'd just be getting to sleep as the light was beginning to break. Through my drowsiness, I heard the crash as Grandma changed back from her bat form before getting off the light fitting, and a few minutes later Mom came into my room to say they were leaving, and to phone her on Pop's carry-it-about phone if we needed to. She also asked if I could clear up the mess at the top of the stairs. Shortly afterwards, I heard the front door opening and then being closed and at that point, exhausted from a restless night, I fell into a deep sleep.

It was almost eleven o'clock when I was awoken by the sound of someone thrashing about in Mom and Pop's bedroom. I was about to investigate when there was a knock on my door.

'Kat,' said Pop urgently, 'I fell asleep when your mom and grandma left. We should have checked on The Hooligoats by now.'

'Okay, Pop, I'll be right down. And don't worry about them, I'm sure they'll be fine.' I don't really know why I said that. I had no idea whether they would be fine or not, mainly because I didn't know what the threat from Ailsa was. Or even if there *was* a threat to the goats, of course.

I got showered and dressed quickly, and went downstairs, where Pop was just finishing a slice of toast.

'Right, I'm ready, Pop. Shall we go?'

Pop nodded and got up.

'Kat?'

'Yes?'

'Well, I don't know why, but I'm not scared. I thought I would be, but I'm not. Whatever is happening, whatever this Ailsa creature is, I'll do my best to protect you. I just wanted you to know that.'

I could have cried when he said that, but I didn't. I just gave him a big hug.

'I know,' was all I could manage, though followed by, 'Now, let's get out there and kick some ass.'

–

I don't know where *let's get out there and kick some ass* came from, honestly. I don't normally stoop to clichés. We made our way round to Pets Corner and found The Hooligoats contentedly chewing hay. All except for Fernando, who was standing with his back to the shed wall, trembling slightly. After all the practice of transmogrifying for the Coming Out party, changing into a Hooligoat had become second-nature to me by now, so I closed my eyes, imagined what I wanted to become and, hey-presto, there I was. A Hooligoat.

'What's eating Fernando?' I asked. 'He looks like he's had a fright.'

Ralph came over. 'Oh, we had old Bogrott, Bossyboots' favourite axeman, round earlier, measuring us up.'

'Measuring you up?' I asked.

'Are you a parrot, or a Hooligoat?' asked Barney.

'You know what I mean,' I said, defensively. 'Why was old Bogrott doing that?'

'He was trying to figure out what size cooking pot he'll need. For when Bossy Barbara gets rid of us.'

'That's not going to happen, I can tell you,' I reassured them. 'We'll think of something, don't you worry.'

Cuthbert joined in. 'We're not worried. Well, okay, Fernie is worried, but he's always worried about something. Bit of a wuss. Old Bogrott has already tried to goatnap

Ralph once. Last year, it was. Thought he could cook Ralph and put him in a freezer for his "Chrissmusdinna". Mr Gohturd gave him a bloody nose.'

'I think you mean kidnap, don't you?' I tried to correct him.

'No, not at all. Goats are only kids until they're one year old. If they're stolen before they're one year old, it's kidnapping, and after that, well it stands to reason that it's goatnapping.'

Pop tried to join in by bleating, 'Is everythig olay, Kap?'

Fernando started giggling.

'Yup, they're okay,' I replied. 'That horrible bloke Bogrott has been round here, menacing poor Fernando.'

'Oh, olay. Well Mr Turdface is in the felt next dool. I'll go and hat a chad with him. Cheek out if Bograt is lackly to be a problob.'

'Mr Turdface?' sniggered Fernando, looking at me. 'Mr Turdface? That's even funnier than Gohturd. Ha ha ha ha.' He promptly fell over with laughter. Still, at least it cheered him up.

'Your pop is getting the hang of Hoolispeak,' said Barney, a tad sarcastically. 'Another few months or so, and he'll be able to ask for some toilet paper to wipe his nose.'

Fernando snorted and rolled around on the floor. 'Turdface,' he spluttered, 'wipe his nose with toilet paper. So funny. Well done Barney.'

I wasn't so amused. 'That's more than a little unkind, Barney,' I scolded him. 'Pop is making a big effort, and there's no other human that can understand Hoolispeak.'

'Oh, yes there is,' said Ralph. 'Bronwen can.'

'Really?' I asked, somewhat surprised. 'But, how do you know that?'

'Well,' explained Ralph, 'last year we organised a birthday party for Mr Turdface, er, sorry, Mr Gohturd. He was going to be by himself for his birthday. We kind of "borrowed" some food from the café and stored it in our shed. Bronwen found it and, when I bleated an apology and explanation to her, she understood what I was saying.'

I was really puzzled. 'But I thought it was just Huldufólk that could understand animal talk. Not humans,' I said, thoughtfully. I wondered whether I needed to mention it to Mom and Grandma.

Cuthbert chipped in, 'She hasn't shown any sign since then that she understands us. Maybe she guessed at what we were saying. Lots of people do. They talk to us as though we're human children. Bronwen was just lucky because she guessed right.'

'Hmmm,' I muttered. 'Still worth checking out, I think.'

Pop came through the side gate and over towards us.

Excitedly, he bleated, 'Mr Turdface thinks Bograt is planning sometiggle.' He looked at Fernando. 'But why is Ferlie robing aroud on the floop?'

Fernie was laughing so much, I thought he wouldn't be able to breathe.

'It's okay, Pop,' I said, kicking Fernando hard in his side. 'It's a stress-release for him. Maybe I'll turn into my human form, again, it'll be easier for you to talk to me.'

'No, no. I'm file, hopelessly, I'm enjoging thif.'

'Well,' I said, speaking slowly and carefully, 'it seems that Bronwen may be able to understand Hoolispeak, which is very odd.'

'Oh dean, that doesly sound left.'

'It doesn't sound right, Pop, not left.'

'Indeelio, indeelio,' Pop said. Then he switched to humanspeak. 'Hmmm, I wish your mom was here, she'd know what to do.'

At that moment Ailsa came through the gate. I'd like to say she walked through but, in reality, she glided as though she were on wheels. Pop stared at her as she stood in front of him and then moved slowly around him, eyeing him up and down as she went. When she'd gone full circle, and was back in front of him, she spoke. Pop seemed unable to move.

'Hello, Reginald.' She rested her hand first on his shoulder, and then moved it up to his cheek. 'It's so nice to see you again.'

'Pop,' I called, 'don't listen to her. POP!'

He didn't respond; he didn't even seem to know I was there. I was tempted to turn back to being a girl, but I thought better of it. Pure instinct, I think.

'I do hope,' Ailsa carried on, 'that those horrid Huldufólk women haven't turned you against me.' She put her finger to her mouth and did a mock-gasp. 'But, oh, that's right. You said you wish that Sarah was here. And I am, Reginald, I'm here. I am Sarah. I am your wife, Sarah, and you must always do what Sarah tells you to. Do you understand me?'

Pop nodded.

'NO, POP, WAKE UP!' I shouted, but I knew there was nothing I could say that Pop would hear. 'Oh, Pop, she isn't Mom, she's some horrible creature. She's Ailsa.'

Just then, there were several men's voices and a lot of clanking, as though chains were being dragged along the floor. The latch on the gate clicked as it was lifted. Ailsa's eyes glowed red, and she hissed, cackled and threw her arms around in anger.

She leaned towards Pop and I heard her whisper, 'I do so hate those sounds. I must go, for now, but I'll be back. I'll see you again soon, my lovely.'

Gliding over to the bushes, she waved her hands slowly in front of her, and a gap opened up. Once she'd floated through it, the gap closed up behind her.

'Pop, we're safe, she's gone. Now, wake up.'

He still didn't move. Then I heard the voice of Ernie Bogrott, who was peering round the corner of the shed at Pop.

Bogrott walked cautiously over to Pop, followed by three other men, all of whom looked every inch as loutish as he did. ''Ee looks loike ee's asleep, but wiv 'is eyes open,' he said to the others.

'Don't touch him,' I bleated, 'or the lads will attack you.' I turned to tell The Hooligoats to do something, only to find that they'd all gone into the shed and were happily munching hay and chatting.

Bogrott came over and peered at me.

''Ere,' he said happily. 'There's anuver o' the likkle blighters nah. Thatun, that red thing, Oi 'avent sid thatun afower.' He gestured for the others to come and look. 'See how the bellies am reeelly big? Lorra meat on 'em. 'Nuff forra few gud meals, Oi fink.'

The four of them came over and looked. One of the others spoke.

''Ere, Ern,' he said, 'why is them fower goats in theer, an thisuns jus standin' theer starin' at us?'

'Dunno, but warrever it is, we need to gerrem outta 'ere quick, afower that bloke werkes up. Come on.'

I didn't know what to do. Should I change back to human, or stay as a goat? Should I run, so that I wouldn't get caught, or stay with the lads? As it happened, I didn't have time to make any decisions. The men had closed in and grabbed me before I could move. They trussed my hooves together with one of the chains and left me lying on my side while they went into the shed and did the same to the others. I called out to Pop, but he just stood there. I was horrified at the thought that Ailsa would be back as soon as the men had carried us out, but there was nothing I could do other than call to him.

'POP, wake up. WAKE UP.'

Nothing. Not even a blink.

The men carried the five of us to the car park where a dirty red open-back truck was parked. They dropped the back panel and tossed each of us onto the piles of rubbish that littered the floor of the truck.

'Well,' I cried, 'fat lot of good you lot were. My pop's been hypnotised by a… a thing. She'll be back, she'll kill him, I know she will.'

Ralph tried to stand, but his hooves were tightly chained, and he just fell back to where he was lying.

'Why? What happened?' asked Barney.

'The Ailsa woman. That thing,' I said, 'whatever she is. She was talking to Pop and he went into a trance. Then I turned round to you lot and you were all in the shed, eating as usual and oblivious to everything else. Then Bogrott came round and she, or it, made a gap in the bushes and disappeared through it.'

'Bogrott?' simpered Fernando. 'What's he going to do with us, as if I didn't know?'

There wasn't any point in keeping the truth from them.

'He's, erm,' I said quietly, 'he's got three other men with him. They were rather interested in how much meat they'd be able to get from us.'

Cuthbert joined in. 'But you can change back to your human form, Kat, you can go and get help.'

'I would if I could, but I'm trussed up the same as you. I can't do anything.'

Just then, Bogrott shouted to the others, 'Oi fink we shud gettoutta 'ere, afower that Gohturd bloke comes back.'

'Too late, Ern,' said one of them. 'Thass 'im coming up the car park.'

'Bogrott,' screamed Mr Gohturd, angrily. 'You villain. What have you got there in the truck?'

'S'all agreed wiv Missus Bradbury. I gets to deal wiv these pesky likkle beggars. We cooks 'em all, an I get to keep one or two of 'em. An' there's fower of us thisstoime, so wot yer gonna do 'baht it?'

'Mrs Bradbury gave us until the end of the month, and we're sure we know how to take them off her hands, so put them back, or I'll…'

'Yule do wot?' jeered Bogrott. 'Anyway, old Bradbury 'as gone into hospital, so she's outta the picture.'

Mr Gohturd's voice lowered. 'If you steal those goats, I guarantee you'll regret it. I'll make sure of that.'

'Yeah? You an' 'ooose army?'

We heard the men getting into the truck, and the engine started. Thick black exhaust smoke covered the back of the truck, and we lay there, coughing and spluttering. As we drove off, the fumes got worse. I looked round at the lads to tell them not to worry, Mr Gohturd would save us, but they had all passed out from the exhaust fumes.

Within seconds, my eyesight blurred, and I fell into a deep, smog-induced sleep.

Chapter Fourteen

Bear Necessities

___

The first thing I remember after that was opening my eyes and seeing Cuthbert lying next to me on a large wooden table, hooves still shackled together. I craned my neck round and could see Barney, Ralph and Fernando. We were all on the same table, which appeared to be at one end of a long barn. Next to the table was a door with a small, dirty glass window in it. I could hear Bogrott and the others, and by stretching my neck in the other direction I could see they were all sitting at a smaller table, drinking a brownish liquid from a bottle which was being passed from one to another.

Bogrott's speech was slurred as he raised the bottle in the air above his head. 'Lessus drink to sum gud fittles. A toast, to the strange likkle goaties wiv the big bellies.'

I'd seen drunken people before, and they were usually not able to move about with any degree of speed, at least not in a straight line. A plan was beginning to hatch in my mind. If only I could wriggle out of the chains that were around my legs, I should be able to make it out of the door.

Then I could change back to human form and run... but that was as far as my thinking went. If Mr Gohturd hadn't been able to stop the four brutes, I thought there was no way I would have the strength to. I'd only be able to save myself, and I wasn't going to leave the lads to face their fate alone.

'We're doomed,' Fernando said to himself.

'Keep your chin up, goat!' ordered Barney.

'What, to make it easier for them to cut my throat?'

Barney didn't answer, and anyway, it all seemed too late. One of the men got unsteadily to his feet.

'Ernie. Oi fink it's toime to git these 'ere critters into the stewin' pot. Oim 'ungry.'

'Yer roight, Jim. Less gerron wiv it.'

I could see them going to a cupboard that was full of sharp-looking knives and choppers. The man called Jim picked up one of the largest knives and walked over to where Cuthbert lay. He stood, swaying from side to side, and raised the knife over his head. As he brought it down, he wobbled, and the blade sliced into the wood right next to Cuthbert's head.

'Ern,' he spluttered. 'Oi fink this bluddy goat keeps movin'. Come an 'old it still willya?'

Ernie stood up, holding on to the table to keep his balance, and was making his way over to help his accomplice when there was a gentle tapping at the window in the door.

'Oo the 'ell is that?' said Jim.

'Goo an' see fer yerself, yer lazy bugger,' said Bogrott. 'An' if it's that Gohturd bloke, tell 'im ter goo away, or we'll punch him on '*is* ooter. See 'ow 'ee loikes it.'

Jim went over to the window and peered through.

''Ere, Ernie,' he said in a puzzled voice. 'It's a bear.'

'A bare wot?'

'Norra bare anyfin', it's a bear. A bluddy big bear by the looks of it, an oi fink it wants ter come in.'

'Yoam jus' drunk, lad. We doh' git bears rahnd 'ere.'

'But oim tellin' yer, Ern. It's a bear.'

'Rubbish, Jim, git outta the way an lemme see, yer drunken fule,' Bogrott bellowed, and started to stagger towards Jim.

Before he could get there, a huge paw suddenly crashed through the glass, and the door flew off its hinges. Jim was flung backwards with the door and lay, dazed, on the floor by the small table. As the dust settled, I could see a large brown bear ambling through the wreckage. It stood up on its hind legs, towering over the men, and roared so loudly I thought my eardrums would burst. The men all screamed and, at first, seemed to be frozen to the spot, but then they ran, picking up Jim and dragging him with them. The bear watched them go, then turned and saw the five of us laid out on the wooden block. It looked us up and down.

'It's measuring us up to see which one to eat first,' cried Cuthbert.

'Think I prefer to have my throat cut,' muttered Fernando. 'At least that would be quicker.'

We all closed our eyes, expecting to be scooped up to become a snack for the bear.

A few moments later came a voice that I recognised.

'Kat, are you okay?'

To say I was stunned would be a serious understatement. 'Bronwen?' I said. 'Is that you?'

''Tis, indeed. Looks like we got here just in time, for sure.'

The bear morphed into Bronwen, and she started to loosen the chains round our legs. As soon as I was free, I quickly changed back to human form.

'We?' I asked.

'Yes, Wilfred came to get me as soon as old Bogrott drove off with you all. He's waiting outside now. He doesn't like to see me when I'm angry.' She smiled and winked. 'Even less when I'm hungry.'

'Wilfred?'

'Wilfred Gohturd.'

'Oh, my. I never even thought of Mr Gohturd having a first name. How silly of me. And you? You're…?'

'Bronwen Beyer, and yes, I'm Huldufólk.'

'Who can change into a…'

'A bear, yes. Canadian grizzly to be exact.'

'Oh,' I said thoughtfully. 'Well, thank you so much for saving us, but I'm confused. Are you telling me that you're Huldufólk, you get to change into a Canadian grizzly, and you've been living in the next village for years without Mom or Grandma knowing?'

'Er. Not quite.'

'Which bit is not quite?'

'The bit about your, erm, grandma not knowing.'

'So Grandma knows, but didn't mention it to me?'

'Ah, yes, see what you mean. Maybe you can get your grandma to explain it when she gets back from Dudley.'

'So you even know where she's gone?'

'Oooh, I do, yes. Oh, dear, I think I ought to explain now that my cover is blown.'

'That,' I said, 'sounds like a good idea.'

'Well, truth is, I'm a C-HYP.'

'A C-HYP?'

'It stands for Commander, Huldufólk Yard Police. It's a bit like Scotland Yard but kind of elvish. I was posted here just after you were born. To keep an eye on you. Make sure you didn't get into any trouble.'

'Er, why? Why would you be sent to watch over me?'

'Ah, the reason why is something I can't tell you. That kind of detail is above my pay-grade, I'm afraid. I do know, though, that I was assigned by your Grandma Finn and the other members of The Elders.'

–

I know! How weird was that? A high-ranking officer, in a police force that I didn't even know existed, had been stationed nearby to watch my back. All I could think was why? Especially when she bakes such superb flapjacks! It suddenly occurred to me that there were huge amounts that I didn't know about Grandma, and the Huldufólk. Despite Grandma's marathon presentation when she'd first arrived.

–

When Bronwen had untied the others, and they were about to jump down from the table, I suddenly remembered.

'POP!' I shouted. 'He'd been hypnotised by that Ailsa thing. She'll kill him.'

'It's okay,' said Bronwen calmly. 'Don't fret. Wilfred saw your father. We got him out of Pets Corner before we came here. If Ailsa went back for him, she'd be disappointed for sure.'

'But, where…'

'He's in the truck outside. He couldn't bear to come in, in case anything had happened to you.'

Fernando suddenly became very animated. 'He couldn't bear it. Ha ha ha, get it? Couldn't bear it? Bear. Y'know, bear? BIG, BIG BEAR?' He started racing round in circles until, exhausted, he collapsed in a heap.

'I think,' said Bronwen, 'that we'll need to carry Fernando back. Looks like it's been a bit too much for him.'

–

We all went outside and there were Pop and Mr Gohturd… Sorry, I can't call him Wilfred, he'll always be Mr Gohturd to me. Besides, what would we have for Fernando to giggle at? So, Pop and Mr Gohturd came running to us, and Pop threw his arms around me.

'Kat, I thought I'd lost you. That vile creature, she, oh I don't know what she did, I just couldn't see or hear anyone but her. It was awful, I'm so sorry I let Bogrott take you. And after I'd said that I'd protect you.'

'Pop, it's okay. I know you couldn't do anything. But are you feeling okay, now?'

'Yes, yes, I'm fine. I could do with getting some fresh air, though, now that I know you're safe.'

Although Bronwen, Pop, and Mr Gohturd had arrived by truck, and despite the fact that daylight was beginning to fade, we all decided to walk along the lane back to Pets Corner. Fernando, who was still fast asleep, was carefully placed in a large rucksack and carried on Mr Gohturd's back. He looked so cute, tucked inside the rucksack like a baby, with his head gently resting on top of Mr Gohturd's shoulder. Barney, Cuthbert and Ralph trotted along just behind us, and we all kept watch for any sign of Ailsa.

'Mr Gohturd?' I said. 'Can I ask you a question?'

'Technically speaking, Kat, you just did.'

I smiled. 'That's the second time someone has said that to me.'

'Sorry, Kat. I'm too clever for my own boots, sometimes. What can I help you with?'

'Don't apologise. Anyway, what I wanted to know is what you meant when you told Bogrott that you were sure you could take The Hooligoats off Bossy Barbara's hands?'

'Ah, right, well, that's an easy one. You know Mrs Purman, who lives at number nine in the high street, next to Pets Corner?'

'Purman? Rings a bell. Oh, yes, you mean Susan!'

'That's right. Sue told us yesterday that she was going to move out of her house this morning. I think she's finding the stairs a bit of a problem since she had that operation for a broken hip, so she's going to live with her daughter in her flat in Cradley Heath. Now, when we told her that we would like to rent her cottage, she was delighted. Bit of income for her, you see, while she's staying with her daughter. I don't know if you've ever been to her cottage, but it's got a huge garden. Huge it is, almost as big as where The Hooligoats live at the moment, and it has a big, big shed to one side. There's even a couple of apple trees, and I know The Hooligoats love the leaves from apple trees so, well it just seems like a perfect solution to us. And Sue is happy for the goats to be there, so long as she doesn't have to clear up the poop, and the best thing of all is that Bronwen and me get to have the goats living with us, in our garden. How fantastic is that?'

Honestly, I was so happy, I could hardly contain my excitement, so I danced a little jig. Not a pretty sight.

'But that's wonderful news, Mr Gohturd, I'm so relieved. I thought the lads were done for.'

'Nah,' said Mr Gohturd, as he reached over his shoulder and scratched behind Fernando's ear. 'Bronwen and me, we couldn't let anything happen to these little fellas, now, could we?'

Fernando started snoring. I smiled to myself, oddly contented.

Pop held my hand tightly all the way down the lane but hardly spoke, preferring instead to stop occasionally to take in deep breaths of clean country air. As we got closer to Pets Corner, though, he suddenly became very tense, as though being close to the farmhouse was affecting him.

'Whatever she did to me, Kat,' he said quietly, 'I know it's in my head. She took over my thoughts. It was as though she was prodding, probing my mind, finding out what I know. I could feel her mind taking control of mine.'

'Pop, try not to worry about it. You need to rest when we get back home, get some sleep.'

'No, I can't sleep, not just now. I'm sure as soon as I sleep she'll be back in my head. And I know it sounds stupid but when she was in my head before, looking at what I was thinking, it was as though *I* could see *her* thoughts as well. Our minds seemed to be connected, both ways. I thought at first that I must have imagined it, dreamt it in some way. But now? Now I'm not so sure. And if I really did see her thoughts, well, we need to do something, and quickly.'

This didn't sound good. 'Why?' I asked tentatively. 'What exactly did you see?'

'I think I saw Mrs Bradbury. In the basement of the farmhouse at Pets Corner. She was tied to a chair.'

'But that's not possible, Pop, Mrs Bradbury went into hospital yesterday. Bogrott said as much.'

'No. She didn't make it. She went into the basement to get some things and disturbed Ailsa, who hit her over the head before tying her up.'

I took a deep breath before asking, 'Disturbed Ailsa? Disturbed her doing what?'

'Marcas was in there, bound to a chair and gagged. I think she was deciding whether or not to kill him.'

Chapter Fifteen

D'yer Need a Hand?

All of us came to a sudden stop, as though we'd walked into a brick wall, and stood staring at Pop. Bronwen was the first to break the silence.

'Are they still alive now?' she asked.

Pop shook his head. 'I don't know. After she'd tied up Mrs Bradbury, she heard something outside the farmhouse. I couldn't make out what it was, but it distracted her, and she went back up to the main farmhouse.'

The thought of Marcas being tied up horrified me. My stomach churned at the possibility that he might even be dead. I felt a desperate panic rising up in me, my legs trembled and I began to sway. Pop held my arm and said something, though his voice seemed like he was standing a long way off.

'Kat, are you okay? Kat?' Pop turned to the others. 'Bronwen, we must call the police, tell them about Marcas and Mrs Bradbury.'

'You forget,' replied Bronwen, 'I am the police, sort of. Now, you take Kat into your cottage…'

'No, wait!' I interrupted.

Everything went quiet as I stood there. I took a deep breath. Then another. And the panic that had immobilised me just a few moments before, started melting away like snow on a spring day, to be replaced by an anger more intense than I'd ever felt before. I stood upright and firm. Then spoke.

'Marcas,' I said through clenched teeth. 'Marcas is MY friend, and I am the ONLY one that can sort this. One way or another.'

As I spoke, my thinking suddenly became so clear, as though a veil had been lifted from my mind.

'Let's all get back to the cottage, we have work to do.'

Pop let go of my arm. 'You have an idea, Kat? A plan?'

'Not yet, but I will have. Now, let's get back home. Damn, I'd forgotten, what can we do about The Hooligoats tonight? I don't fancy leaving them at Pets Corner.'

'Just for tonight,' said Pop. 'Just for tonight they can stay in our garage. Just for tonight, mind.'

As Pop, Mr Gohturd, and The Hooligoats set off ahead of us, I turned to Bronwen. 'Pop can't be trusted, unfortunately. If Ailsa managed to get inside his head, she may still be able to know anything that he knows.' Bronwen nodded, as I carried on in a whisper. 'We have technology on our side, so I'd like to check the internet to see if we can find out anything about Ailsa. I've seen what she does to men, and the likelihood is that she was responsible for what happened to Mr Brown. But I'll need you to stay with Pop and Mr Gohturd when I go to find Marcas.'

Bronwen shook her head. 'I must come with you, I'm trained for hostage situations,' she said.

I looked hard at her. 'When I met Ailsa, she said that she could see me,' I explained. 'I think she meant that she could see that I'm Huldufólk. And if she knows about me, she'll know about you, so we can't go there in human form. But when I was a Hooligoat, that was different, she didn't pay me any attention, she didn't even seem to realise I was there. If I go there as a goat, I'm hoping she won't know it's me.'

Bronwen was unconvinced. 'So I could go in as a bear.'

'No, that won't work. At least, as a goat, I can sneak in without her seeing me, but a bear would be spotted easily. No. It has to be me, just me.'

'But I'm charged with looking after you, Kat. I can't leave you to do this alone. Why don't we wait until your mom and grandma are back?'

'Because we can't wait. We have to strike now and hope that Marcas and Mrs Bradbury are still alive. If we delay it, and she kills them, I'll never forgive myself.'

Bronwen shrugged. 'You're right,' she said. 'I know you are, but I feel that I should be doing this, not having you risking your life.'

'I have to do this, Bronwen. If you want to help, then go and watch over Pop and Mr Gohturd and the lads. If I fail, if I don't come back, I'd like to think they're safe.'

—

It didn't take long on the computer. Once I'd put "Female Scottish Monster" into the search engine, I came up with a number of possibilities. Further research narrowed it down, until there was just one that seemed to fit what I had witnessed Ailsa doing to Pop AND what appeared to have happened to Mr Brown.

I stared intently at the screen and read quietly to myself. 'B-A-O-B-H-A-N – S-I-T-H, pronounced *Baa'vaan shee*.'

'Oh dear,' I muttered. 'She's a vampire!'

–

There were so many questions that I didn't have the answer to but, at that particular moment, none of them seemed to matter. If I was right, the only proven defence would be something made of iron. And, of course, that figured. Ailsa had fled when Bogrott and his chums came through the gate with a load of old chains. The links must have been made of iron.

I explained what I'd learned to Bronwen, keeping well out of earshot of Pop and Mr Gohturd.

'Look,' I said quietly, 'I think this creature Ailsa is probably a Baobhan Sith, a fairly vicious kind of vampire. They can use the fact that someone, usually male, says that he's missing someone else as an invitation to engage with them and kill them so, whatever happens, don't let Pop or Mr Gohturd say anything that might give her permission to enter the house.'

Bronwen nodded, then made one more attempt to persuade me to wait, but I'd made my mind up. There was no stopping me, I just needed to get it done.

I searched in the house for a torch, but the only one

I could find was a small thin one, like a pencil, in the kitchen drawers. I made sure it worked, then popped into the garage to check on The Hooligoats. Fernando was still fast asleep, and the others were busy pulling hay out of some netting that Mr Gohturd had rigged up for them.

I took an extra-deep breath and left the house, making my way to Pets Corner. As soon as I got close, I shape-shifted to goat form and edged my way round towards the farmhouse, with the unlit torch held firmly in my mouth. I'd hoped getting in through the back door would be easier. With it being such an old farmhouse, I also hoped that I would find some iron on the way.

Although daylight had gone, it was cloudless and there was quite a bright moon shining down. As I cautiously dashed from one bush to another, trying to keep out of sight as much as possible, I suddenly realised I could hear people blundering around. And the sounds were coming from just by The Hooligoats' shed. Staying behind the trees, I made my way round towards the noise.

'Where've the likkle beggars got to, Ernie?'

'Dunno, Jim, they shud be in 'ere. We sawed 'em comin' dahn the road, din't us?'

'Praps that bear 'ad 'em fer dinna, matey.'

Bogrott sounded irritated. 'Nah. I tell yer, we wus delooshnul. We'd jus'ad too much wisky, thassall. There ain't any bears rahnd ere. Blimee Jim, yoam gerrin' on me nerves. I dow arf miss yower bruver. I wish 'ee wus 'ere. 'Eed got muwer sense in is likkle finger than yow 'ave in yer 'ole 'and.'

I couldn't help thinking that Bogrott's wish was not something he should be voicing out loud, and I was right.

Within seconds, there was a gentle swooshing sound.

'Oh, 'allo theyer miss. Now, weyer did yow come from?'

'You must be Earnest Bogrott,' crooned Ailsa. 'I've heard so much about you. And who are your lovely friends?'

I eased myself round so that I could see what was happening. Bogrott was standing with the other three ruffians, and Ailsa was hovering gently in front of them. Bogrott introduced his chums to her.

'Well, miss, this is Jimmy Tuff... and Tommy Tangler... and this 'ere is Stanley Cherry.'

'How wonderful to meet you all, you keep such pleasant company, Earnest,' said Ailsa. 'Now, I'd like all of you to pay close attention to my eyes, please.'

'Yes, miss, and wot luvly eyes yuve g...'

The four of them stood quite still, looking straight ahead.

'Hmmm,' murmured Ailsa, as she licked her lips with a long black tongue, 'you all look quite delicious. But I can't eat all of you right now. Maybe I'll just manage one, and save the others for another day. But I'm spoiled for choice, so which one shall I have?'

She wafted around and in between them, examining, prodding arms and legs, pinching flesh. She finally settled in front of Stanley.

'I think you'll do nicely,' she hissed. 'Nice chubby belly, plenty of meat. Yes, I think I'd like a bite or two of this particular Cherry.'

With her face close to his, she grasped his chin and tugged down so that his mouth was open, then opened her own mouth and breathed in long and deep. A greenish vapour spiralled out of Stanley's mouth and into hers. As she continued to breathe in, her hands began to change, her nails growing longer and longer like talons, her fingers stretching further and further, until they wrapped round Stanley's neck. This went on for a few moments, then Stanley began to crumple to the floor. But as he started to fold, Ailsa held him up and threw her head back.

'Cor,' said a hushed voice behind me, 'haven't seen fangs like that since your mom turned into a weirdwolf that Sunday.'

I spun round. 'Ralph, what on... Barney, Cuthbert? You're all supposed to be at home with Pop, Bronwen and Mr Gohturd. And, for your information, Mom doesn't have fangs, she has canines, and she's not a werewolf. Or a weirdwolf for that matter. Now go home, it's too dangerous here.'

Barney shook his head. 'You had the chance to escape when Bogrott had captured us,' he said, 'but you didn't. You stayed with us. Now we're going to stay with you, no matter what the danger.'

'Yes, and anyway,' added Cuthbert, 'you're one of us, now. You're family.'

I felt so touched by that. 'Oh, that's lovely of you to say so. Thank you, boys.'

'So,' asked Ralph, 'what's the plan?'

'I don't have a plan as such,' I had to admit. 'I was kind of playing it by ear.'

Ralph looked intently at me. 'I dunno,' he whispered. 'First you're *all* ears, then you're *playing it* by ear. You're fixated on ears, Kat Hooligoat.'

I laughed, quietly. 'Thank you for those kind words, Ralph. Now, I need to find some iron, and a way in.'

'Can I suggest, then,' said Cuthbert, 'that we make our way to the secret door? That's got some old iron bars in front of it, and we can stand guard while you go and get Marcas and Bossyboots.'

I suppose I shouldn't have been surprised. 'So, there's a secret door in the farmhouse as well as the shed AND the café?'

'Course there is. Come on and we'll show you. And get a move on, before fangyface realises we're here.'

—

After making sure that Ailsa was still busy with poor Stanley, we made our way a little further round, to where a large bush covered part of the side of the house. Barney held the branches to one side, and Ralph led the way through. There, overgrown with moss and lichen was a small wooden door, in front of which was a rusty old iron poker.

'This door opens straight onto the stairs that lead down to the basement. Once upon a time it was used by delivery men when they took sacks of coal to where the furnace is,' Cuthbert whispered as he pushed one of his horns into the gap between the door and the frame and levered the door open.

I poked my head through the opening. It was dark inside. I changed back to human form, grabbed the poker, and switched on the torch. As I shone the light inside, I could see a thick mist swirling about on the floor. I didn't like to think of what may be lurking around within it.

'Marcas,' I whispered, 'are you there?'

Everything was eerily silent. I panned the little torch round in an arc, hoping, almost against hope, that it would pick out Marcas. And, at last, against the far wall I spotted a solitary chair on which was slumped a figure, blindfolded and gagged. My heart leapt for joy as the figure gave a muffled grunt. It was Marcas.

With the dense mist oozing coldly round my legs, I gingerly made my way down the steps and towards the chair. As I reached Marcas, I lifted the blindfold up over his head, then tugged hard at the tape that was stuck across his mouth.

'OUCH,' he cried out.

'Sssssh,' I muttered urgently. 'Don't make a sound, or she'll hear us. Is Mrs Bradbury here?'

'Thank goodness you're here, Ginger Kat, and no she isn't,' whispered Marcas. 'Now, please, please, can you untie me so we can get out of here before that monster comes back?'

I reached round to the back of the chair, carefully feeling along the ropes until I found the knots, which lay beneath the surface of the mist. They were fastened tightly.

'It's no good,' I whispered. 'I can't undo the knots. I'm going to have to find something to cut the rope.'

I shone the torch round the walls, but could see nothing that might help. Just then, I felt something brush against my knees. Something furry. I shone the torch downwards, and looked in horror as a pair of horns gradually emerged into the light.

'Hallo,' bleated Ralph, quietly. 'You're taking a long time, d'yer need a hand?'

'Ralph,' I breathed. 'You startled me, creeping about like that. And, unless you happen to have a knife that will cut through rope, then it's probably best if you wait outside with the others.'

'No worries, we're always chewing things and you never know, rope might taste even better than hay.'

Ralph dived into the mist, and I could hear him steadily chomping away. It only took him about a minute to chew through the rope, during which time both Marcas and I stared anxiously at the doorway at the top of the steps. But then, the ropes dropped free and Marcas tried to stand.

'Owww,' he muttered under his breath. 'I cut my leg when that thing dragged me down here. It's been bleeding quite badly.'

'Lean on me, I'll try to support you. We really do need to get out of here though, Marcas, bloodied leg or not.'

With help, Marcas was able to hobble up the steps, but at the top he stopped and gasped in pain. I thought he was going to pass out.

'The wheelbarrow,' I muttered to myself. 'I left it just round the corner after we carted Pop home in it.'

I propped Marcas up against the wall, with Ralph and Barney standing by him to stop him from falling, then eased my way round the corner of the farmhouse. The barrow was still where I'd left it. As quietly as I could, I wheeled it round and positioned it next to Marcas who, by now, was looking very shaky.

'I'm afraid it's not a very dignified way to travel, Marcas, but it'll have to do.'

With the three goats doing their bit to nudge Marcas along, I heaved him into the barrow.

By the time we were ready to make our escape, Barney started hopping from hoof to hoof, then put his head down and tried to push me along.

'For goodness' sake, let's go,' he bleated. 'She must be down to Stanley's toenails by now.'

Urged on by the three Hooligoats, I managed to push the wheelbarrow out as far as the lane. As soon as we got onto tarmac, Barney, who was bringing up the rear, started nudging into my legs again.

'Can I suggest, please, that we RUN?'

And we did. Fast. Wheelbarrow and all.

—

We arrived back at the cottage just in time to see Mom's car pull up on the driveway, which was bathed in light from the outside lamps over the garage. Making a final dash, we raced onto the drive just as Mom and Grandma were getting out of the car.

'Mom, Grandma,' I gushed. 'Bogrott captured me and the lads but Bronwen Bear saved us, then we rescued Marcas. Ailsa was going to kill him, she tried to kill Pop and she's just killed one of Bogrott's men. We saw her, she was eating...'

But Mom and Grandma weren't looking at us. They were looking past us, and up the lane.

'Er,' I whispered, 'she's behind us, isn't she?'

Chapter Sixteen

Horseshoes

———

Grandma nodded slowly as she opened the back door of the car and dragged out a large box, which clanged onto the drive. All the time she kept her eyes on the lane behind us.

I turned round just in time to see Ailsa emerge from the darkness, the redness of her eyes burning bright, her fangs dripping with blood, tatters of clothing hanging from her talons.

'Could you all,' Grandma said, calmly and quietly, 'step behind me, please, and keep close together?'

'I thought you'd never ask,' replied Ralph, moving faster than I'd ever seen him move before.

When we were all behind her, Grandma opened the box and took out a number of old horseshoes, which she laid out in a long row on the drive in front of her. Ailsa glided towards us, stopping just at the edge of the drive.

'Give the boy back to me,' she hissed, rubbing her hands together. 'I must have him. He needs more fattening up, but he'll be a tasty young morsel when he's ready.'

Marcas sat up in the barrow. 'I wondered why there was so much cake and pastries,' he said. 'I thought Bronwen must have been doing too much baking.'

'Let me have him and I'll let the rest of you go free.'

'That's not going to happen, and you know it,' said Grandma firmly.

'Then I will kill all of you. Your bodies will provide a banquet for my family. When my sisters get here, we will feed on your bones until we are ready to hibernate once more.'

'Oh, I think not.'

Ailsa seethed, 'Even Huldufólk magic is no match for mine, old woman. I will destroy you.'

Grandma stood her ground without even twitching. 'My magic may not be powerful enough for you,' she pointed at the horseshoes, 'but these are.'

Ailsa looked down at the row of horseshoes, and started to move rapidly towards us.

'They are nothing,' she screeched. 'They are just…' She stopped suddenly.

'Iron,' I said, knowingly, as Grandma gave me a look of approval. 'I think that's the word you were looking for,' I continued. 'They are iron horseshoes. And your kind can't stand iron, can you?'

Ailsa spun around in fury like a whirlwind, and backed away a short distance. She stopped spinning. Words spat out from her mouth.

'You will pay for this. All Huldufólk will pay for this, with their miserable lives.'

Grandma spoke again. 'You've tried that before, if I

remember correctly, in the Highlands of Scotland it was. Your home turf, supposed to be. Long, long time ago. We defeated you then, and we'll defeat you again. You and your sisters will be back in custody before you know it, so stick that in your pipe and smoke it.'

Ailsa suddenly stopped and stood still, as though she was listening carefully to something. Then she pointed a long bony claw at Grandma.

'We will return,' she laughed.

'We'll be waiting,' replied Grandma. 'And we'll be ready.'

In the blink of an eye, we were left staring as Ailsa shape-shifted into a wolf and sat howling at the moon before running away up the lane.

'Shall I go after her?' asked Mom.

'No,' replied Grandma. 'She's right, I'm afraid. Her magic is more powerful than ours. And when she's with her sisters... well, we'll need to be prepared, and that's all there is to it.'

Curiosity got the better of me again. 'Just as a matter of interest,' I wanted to know, 'how many sisters has she got?'

'So long as they haven't added to their numbers, there's three in addition to Ailsa, so four of them altogether. Strictly speaking, one of them isn't actually her sister. More of a mother, really.'

Grandma seemed to relax. 'But I think she's gone for now, so let's all get indoors. That goes for The Hooligoats too, they can stay in the garage for now. And I think a cup of tea and some biscuits are in order.'

I didn't think it was worth mentioning that the goats

had already been in the garage. 'Okay, but Mom, you'll need to move the car so that I can open the garage doors to let the lads through,' I said.

'No, it's okay,' Mom replied. 'They can go into the house and through the connecting door in the kitchen.' She looked down at the lads and smiled broadly at them. 'Provided they don't POOP on the way.'

The Hooligoats looked up fearfully. 'Yes, miss,' they chorused.

—

Ten minutes later, we were all crowded into the living room in the cottage. Mr Gohturd, Bronwen and Pop had witnessed the standoff with Ailsa through the living room windows, and excitedly congratulated us all on our rescue of Marcas, and for then standing up to Ailsa.

Mom started to dress the wound on Marcas' leg. He was still quite woozy, and I'd made him rest on the settee. As he lay there, I think he suddenly realised he was safe, and grabbed my hand.

'Ginger Kat,' he said, weakly. 'I owe you my life. I'd seen what that monster could do, and I knew what she was capable of, but you found me, and you risked your own life to save me. Thank you.'

'You saw what she was?' I asked.

Marcas nodded. 'That Sunday, the day after we'd been to Wenlock Priory, I went back to Pets Corner after we'd been there on the morning. I hid in the bushes so that I could jump out and startle you. I saw the whole thing.'

'The whole thing?'

'Everything. I was about to jump out when that strange thing emerged from the elderflower bush and talked to you about the ARK. Then I saw you turn into a Hooligoat. I couldn't believe what I was watching, and when your mother arrived and became a wolf I, well I thought that was about as weird as things could get. I didn't really know what to do, so I sneaked out of the bushes and was about to set off home, when I stumbled on that thing, whatever she is. She was bending over the body of a man. I couldn't recognise him. Not that there was much of him left to recognise. She ripped off his arm, and started to chew on it. I must have stepped on a twig or something, because that's when she flew at me. Before I knew it, I was tied up, being force-fed cake and stuff. And my leg hurt like crazy. I honestly thought it was the end for me. I hoped and hoped for someone to find me. I'm glad it was you.'

I squeezed his hand, and he squeezed mine in return.

'Thank you,' he said, as he lapsed into sleep.

—

As we all sat, quietly talking and trying not to wake Marcas, there was a gentle knocking on the door that led from the kitchen and into the garage.

'Can pygmy goats learn to knock on a door like that?' asked Pop, nervously.

'I wouldn't have thought so,' said Grandma. 'I'll go and check. Everyone else stay just where you are.'

We all froze and held our breath. It didn't take long for Grandma to return, though she had a very puzzled look on her face. She spoke hesitantly.

'It was Fernando. I don't understand why, but he wanted me to ask specifically for a Mr Turdface to go and say goodnight.'

As she finished speaking, there was a loud outburst of merriment from the garage.

Kids!

Chapter Seventeen

Ice Prisons

—

O nce Mr Gohturd had settled the goats down again, Grandma tapped on her cup to get everyone's attention.

She turned and looked straight into my eyes. 'So, Kat. Bronwen Bear eh?' she said.

I suddenly realised that blurting everything out in the street may not have been the right approach, so I recounted the events of the day to Grandma and Mom. At least up to the point of being rescued from Bogrott and his chums. Fortunately, Bronwen joined in at the end.

'Sorry, ma'am,' she said, 'I had no choice, I'm afraid. Once Bogrott had kidnapped them, I had to go in as a bear, or risk having him kill them all.'

Grandma was more understanding than I'd expected. 'I know. And of course you did, Officer. You did the right thing. That's exactly why you were posted to keep an eye on things.'

'Yes, Bronwen,' joined in Mom, 'Grandma told me

about you when we were on the way back. You did a grand job. Well done and thank you.'

'It was nothing, ma'am, thank you.'

Mom has never been too keen on formalities. 'There's no need to call me ma'am, Bronwen. The name is Sarah.'

Bronwen bobbed her head slightly to Mom. 'Yes ma'am. Sorry, yes Sarah.'

'Same goes for me,' said Grandma, 'I'm not keen on ma'am either. The name is Grandma.'

I remember thinking it was probably not the right time to say it, but I said it anyway, 'Grandma, Bronwen wasn't posted here to keep an eye on *things*, was she? She was posted here to keep an eye on *me*. And I don't understand why.'

'I'm sure you don't, Kat,' replied Grandma with a deadpan look on her face. 'That's why I'm about to tell you.'

I couldn't hide my astonishment. 'Are you?'

'Of course I am. I don't believe in keeping secrets, you know. At least not unless it's something that folk shouldn't know about. But, anyway, before I go into all that, let's talk about Ailsa. I was going to tell everyone what she is, but I have a feeling that you already know, Kat.'

'Well, I think she a Baobhan Sith, a vampire,' I volunteered.

'Well done, Kat. And you're right. Ailsa is as old as the hills. She's a Scottish vampire, usual habitat, in fact, is the Highlands of Scotland, though they have been known to move around at times.'

'What?' Mr Gohturd wanted to know. 'A vampire as in Dracula-neck-biting-blood-sucking type vampire?'

'Oh, much, much worse, I'm afraid. The Baobhan Sith are so vicious that Dracula would be more than happy to swap his fangs for dentures to have one of these creatures in his pack. Let alone four of them.'

Mr Gohturd looked puzzled. 'So why is she here?' he asked.

'We only have our suspicions about her presence in the village, but you remember me mentioning a business trip to Scotland that was a bit messy?'

'Yes.'

'Well, Ailsa was the reason why the trip was messy, because I went there as part of a team of Elders to capture her. Only, she didn't have a name then.' Grandma took the last biscuit from the second tray before continuing, 'They've existed almost as long as Huldufólk have. Just like us, they are all female, and just like us, they can shape-shift. But, whereas Dracula and his cronies turn into bats, Baobhan Sith prefer wolves. And before you ask, Kat, not even your mom would be a real match for them.'

Bronwen chimed in, 'What about me? Grizzlies must stand a good chance, for sure?'

'I'm afraid not. The two of you might be able to slow them down if you work together, but the Baobhan Sith are cruel, violent, and, well, just plain evil. The only thing that seems to work against them is iron.'

'I know!' I shouted, probably louder than I needed to. 'So, is iron what you used to catch them?' I asked.

'Iron, that's right, but back then there was quite a big team of us, and we knew roughly where all of them were, so we could lay iron traps for them. At the moment, we know where Ailsa is, but none of the others.'

'And is iron what you use to kill them?' asked Mr Gohturd.

Grandma shook her head. 'The only ways we found to kill them was by piercing the heart, or decapitating them.'

I picked up the trail. 'So you actually *did* manage to kill some of them?'

'Yes. Originally there were seven sisters and, for some reason, they'd taken up residence in some caves just the other side of Dudley.'

I nearly jumped off my seat. 'The Seven Sisters cavern, in the Wren's Nest. Was that it? That area is on Wenlock limestone and it's got loads and loads of fossils in it. It's a nature reserve and geosite now, and the caves were used as openings to mine shafts. They've been partly filled in now because the roofs were unsafe.'

'Yesss,' said Grandma, looking slightly suspiciously at me. 'How do you know about that?'

'Geography, we went there on a field-trip last year. I do pay attention, you know.'

'Hmmm, you do, don't you?'

Something else suddenly dawned on me. I was on fire that night. 'But aren't we forgetting?' I said. 'If you captured them before, how come they're wandering about now? Did they get released on bail, or have their sentence reduced for good behaviour, or something?'

'Wondered if you'd pick up on that, Kat. Truth is that they were imprisoned deep down in ice, frozen they were, way down in the polar ice cap. Problem is, the ice cap has receded to a point where they've been thawed out.'

'They've escaped because the planet is warming up?' I said incredulously.

'That's about it,' admitted Grandma.

'Ailsa has gone.' Pop had been quiet so far, but this contribution came as a bit of a bombshell. 'When you all came into the house, I could feel her still inside my head. I could sense where she was. Now, there's nothing at all. She's gone.'

'Oh dear,' Grandma said, almost to herself. 'I suppose that figures.'

'Why so?' I demanded. 'She was fattening up Marcas for when her sisters got here. AND she was keeping Bogrott, and two of his friends, for supper. Why would she just disappear?'

'Well,' replied Grandma thoughtfully, 'Baobhan Sith differ from ordinary vampires in that they only rise to feed once a year. Interestingly, they mainly attack men, who they invariably kill and eat, after first hypnotising them and sucking the lifeforce out of them. On rare occasions they have been known to attack women but, when they have, they seem to be able to bite them in such a way that the victim becomes one of them.'

Pop asked, 'So why did she leave, with food still in the larder, so to speak?'

'We think that Ailsa escaped from the ice before the others, so she may have got here first and needed to feed after being imprisoned for such a long time. In which case, it's possible that her sisters made contact telepathically with her and she's gone now to join up with them.'

'She did look as though she was listening to something when we were on the drive,' I said. 'But when will they come back?'

Grandma shrugged. 'Could be anytime, that's if they come back here at all, we just don't know what their plans might be. Assuming they have plans, of course. It may be that we just have to wait until there are more reports of deaths that look like animal attacks.'

'Whoopee do,' I exclaimed, with perhaps a hint of sarcasm. 'Well, they like to be invited in before they kill, so why don't we invite them to my birthday party?'

'Oh, goodness,' cried Pop, 'it's your birthday on Sunday. I'd completely forgotten with everything that's going on.'

'Don't worry, Pop,' I consoled him. 'I think birthdays are at the bottom of the list of priorities right now.'

'Anyway,' said Grandma, 'we're now having to re-assess all the other polarprisons that were used to house the various monsters, so that we can make sure they're not breached. Of course, that assessment may not be as comprehensive as it should have been because someone, and I'm not naming names, mind, but someone has mislaid the maps of where the prisons were. Not that I think I had them in the first place, you understand.'

Being as Grandma had promised to tell us about it, I thought the time had come to ask the big question.

'Grandma,' I said as calmly as I could. 'Is the reason that Bronwen was watching over me something to do with all this stuff about monsters?'

'Hmm,' Grandma replied. 'Your brain is in gear tonight isn't it?'

'So?'

'Yes, at the beginning at least. But, now, we believe there's actually no link between you and the monsters.'

That was too deep for me. 'I don't understand,' I said.

'Well, I need to tell you about The Prophecy.'

'The Prophecy?' Mom said, her face going very red. 'What prophecy?'

'I don't suppose you'd know about it, Sarah, but it exists, nonetheless. As it happens, I can tell you all about it now, because The Elders are not sure it's a valid document.'

'Go on.'

'No-one knows how The Prophecy came to be part of Huldufólk heritage. It seems like it's always been there. It forecast the coming of evil, although it didn't say what the evil would be, just that it would be resurrected by the deeds of mankind.'

If anything, Mom seemed to blush an even deeper shade of red.

Grandma continued, 'And it said that a Huldufólk child would be born, with hair the colour of fire, and—'

'Is that me?' I asked.

'Maybe, but we don't think so now. When you were born, there was a possibility that it was you, and that's why you were guarded by Bronwen, but that turned out not to be the case.'

'Confusing,' I said. 'But how do you know that?'

'Because it said that this child, the one with hair the colour of fire, would be able to rise up into the air on the wings of an eagle, and have the body of a lion.'

'A gryphon,' I said, excitedly. 'And I was meant to be a gryphon.'

'Technically speaking, Kat,' interrupted Marcas, drowsily, 'I think a gryphon has the body of a lion from the waist down. Above that, it has the body of an eagle.'

Everyone looked round at Marcas who, until now, had been fast asleep.

Grandma was undeterred. 'If you were really meant to be a gryphon,' she gave Marcas a sidelong glance, 'or anything even remotely resembling a gryphon, you wouldn't have been able to become a Hooligoat. The ARK would have known that, and would have helped you to fulfil your true destiny. *If* you were the child mentioned in The Prophecy, that is. But you're not. And none of us even know for sure that this particular time, the rise of these monsters, is actually the one that The Prophecy refers to.'

Despite the way that Grandma had looked at him, Marcas bravely spoke again. 'Can I ask a question?' he said.

Quick as a flash, I answered, 'Technically speaking, Marcas, you just did.'

Marcas seemed to ignore my bit of silliness. 'I'd like to know why you say that the Baobhan Sith turn into wolves. Isn't it possible that she's primarily a wolf that turns into a Baobhan Sith?'

I thought that was a valid question, a sign of a mind that questions everything. Grandma just raised her eyebrows and tutted.

And that was it for the evening. Almost. Mom and Pop sorted out who was sleeping where, and Grandma once again said she'd hang guard for the night, being as she was the nocturnal one. Everyone made their way to their respective beds, but I stayed back. I just wanted to ask one last question about The Prophecy. I suppose, in a way, I wanted it to be about me.

'Are you sure, Grandma, that the child mentioned isn't me?'

'As sure as I can be, Kat,' said Grandma, giving me a hug. 'The child in The Prophecy would have become our Warrior Queen, one who would lead us in our fight against evil. You can't do that as a Hooligoat, no matter how mischievous Hooligoats may be. There's also the fact that Ailsa has gone away.'

'What's that got to do with it?'

'We suspect… actually we are fairly certain, that she came to the village because she thought that the Warrior Queen might be here. The Warrior Queen being someone who, at a specific point, would be able to harness the tremendous powers of Mother Earth, and destroy the Baobhan Sith. Ailsa would want to kill the Queen before she was able to harness those powers, but she obviously didn't think you were a threat to her because she didn't see you as the Queen. So, she's gone. Now, I know what you did today, rescuing Marcas and—'

'But, how do you know that?' I spluttered. 'I haven't told you about it yet.'

'Oh, that's true. At least, it's true that you haven't told me anything about it out loud but, remember what I said about being able to *see* what someone is thinking? And I see you, Kat. I see you so very clearly. You went into that basement, knowing what Ailsa was doing to Stanley and you found Marcas, despite the fact that it was so frightening. Then you rescued him, and the only help that you had was from The Hooligoats. You may not be able to shape-shift into a gryphon and have the body of a lion, but you have the courage of one, and that's as good a start as any. And, when the time comes for you to soar, I just know you'll rise to the challenge.'

—

I remember feeling so happy that Grandma had recognised how difficult it had been for me to rescue Marcas. I don't think I felt brave when I went into the basement, though. I simply knew what had to be done. Or, rather, it's not that I *knew* what had to be done, it was more instinct than knowledge. Maybe, at that point, I was beginning to connect with Mother Earth after all.

I do suppose now, though, looking back on what Grandma said that night, the way she kept side-tracking me, and the words she used, I should have known even then that she wasn't telling me the whole truth about The Prophecy.

Chapter Eighteen
A Plan is Born

＿＿＿

On the following day, before we could start thinking about how to deal with the Baobhan Sith, we had some tidying-up to do.

Pop phoned Marcas' parents, who dropped everything and raced round to our cottage. There were lots of questions, but Marcas couldn't really tell anyone the detail of what had actually happened, mainly because he was sure no-one would believe him, so he took the sensible way out. He told his parents simply that he'd been blindfolded and gagged and couldn't say where he'd been kept. And, although Marcas' parents were delighted that he was safe and sound, he was adamant that he wanted to stay with us for the time being. I must say, if it was me that had gone missing, Mom and Pop wouldn't let me out of their sight again, but Marcas' parents agreed quite readily. I wonder if that's a boy thing?

The police, who turned up shortly afterwards, were told the same thing and, to be honest, they were much more concerned about the fact that there had been at least one more vicious murder, perhaps two, in the village. Poor Stanley had been pretty much completely devoured. All that was left of him was one of his big toes and a partly chewed ear. His bloodied clothing, or rather patches of it, was found strewn around the car park. His chums, Bogrott, Jim and Tommy, were taken in for questioning, though we didn't expect them to be charged. And there was no sign at all of Bossy Barbara, beyond a small patch of blood that was found in the kitchen in the farmhouse, which police believed was hers.

As had happened when Marcas had disappeared and Mr Brown had been murdered, there was a great deal of activity through the day but, in essence, the police appeared to be completely baffled by events. We weren't much further forward either, and it seemed like the Baobhan Sith had the upper hand. Only they would know if, and when, they would return to the village. All we could do, we thought, was to keep an eye out for deaths that might indicate where they were. That particular thought, of course, was destined to change very quickly.

–

Not wanting to pass up on the fact that Marcas had held my hand the previous evening, I insisted on taking him for a hobble to Pets Corner just after lunch. And, yes, we held hands again. Just so that Marcas would be able to walk more easily, you understand.

Mom and Pop had agreed not to relocate The Hooligoats to Sue Purman's garden, but to keep them with us for the time being so, once Marcas had limped a short way along the lane and back again, we went into the garage to spend some time with the lads.

Marcas and I chatted about my Huldufólk heritage, and my ability to shape-shift into a pygmy goat. We even managed to have a laugh about the way that Ralph had risen up out of the mist in the basement. And, inevitably, the conversation turned to the Baobhan Sith. I tried to explain the issues to Marcas.

The first problem, I told him, was that we needed to make sure that Ailsa and her sisters came back to our village, instead of restricting their hunting to wherever they happened to be. If The Elders were right, Ailsa had come to find the Warrior Queen so that she could destroy her but, as she'd decided that I wasn't the Queen, she'd lost interest in being around me.

Secondly, even if we could induce them to come back to the village, we would then need to lure them into a trap. As there were four of them, we would be risking the lives of four men who would have to act as bait. Pop and Mr Gohturd had volunteered to do the luring, and that was very brave of them, but Pop had already been "connected" with Ailsa, and she'd be able to read his mind quite easily. Grandma actually thought she might be able to do a spell that would shield Pop's mind, but she couldn't be certain that Ailsa would be unable to break through it.

So, all in all, our task appeared to be impossible. Until Ralph, who'd obviously been listening in, piped up.

'There's four of us,' he said enthusiastically. 'We can do the luring. We can get those Bobby Sif things into a trap.'

'Thanks for the suggestion, Ralph,' I replied, after translating what Ralph had said so that Marcas could understand. 'But it wouldn't work. Ailsa took no notice of me when I was a goat. She only did when I was in human form.'

'Then make us all human. We heard you talking to Grandma about doing that. You could make us your Familiars and give us human form. Ailsa would take notice of us then. And, when the Bobby Sif all came in, we could change back to being Hooligoats and escape by running straight between their legs. Kaboom. They'd be too surprised to stop us. We could lure 'em into the basement in the farmhouse.'

'Okaaaay,' I mused. 'Assuming I could get permission from The Elders to have four Familiars…'

'No problemnibus,' said Cuthbert, chewing some hay. 'Nashinole mergency and all that.'

'Yeeesss,' I continued. 'So you four could lure them to the basement, but how would we get them to come here to the village in the first place? After all, Ailsa doesn't think I'm the Warrior Queen.'

We all stood and pondered, and then it struck me. 'Unless…' I said.

'Unless what?' asked Marcas.

I started to get quite excited myself. 'Unless I *were* to be the Warrior Queen. That would get them here, wouldn't it?'

'But you're not the Warrior Queen,' said Barney. 'Or are you?'

'No, I'm not. But Ailsa doesn't know that. Not for sure, she doesn't. And if I'm crowned, in a big ceremony with lots of Huldufólk in attendance, that should persuade her enough to get her here. And Pop will know if she gets close. He'll be able to sense her mind.'

'Well, sounds like we've got a plan,' Fernando said.

'There's a few things to sort out but, yes, we sure have the makings of one. Thank you, boys.'

–

I could hardly contain myself when we walked back through to the cottage, but there were parts of the plan that I needed to get clear in my head before divulging it to Mom, Grandma, Pop, Bronwen and Mr Gohturd. I knew I needed to take some quality time to think.

But, then again, when did "need" ever override excitement? Just five minutes later, despite Marcas subtly shaking his head, I couldn't keep the idea to myself.

'I think I know how we can get the Baobhan Sith safely into custody,' I announced.

Grandma was the only one who didn't look up in astonishment. She actually seemed to be expecting it.

'Go on,' she said. 'You'll have thought it all through very carefully by now, I presume?'

'Er, yes, something like that. Anyhow, it started with something that Ralph suggested, and it just all seemed to fall into place from there.'

'I do hope,' remarked Pop, 'that it's not one of Ralph's more outlandish ideas? I've heard about his project for flying pigs.'

'No, not at all. It's actually really simple.'

'Well,' suggested Grandma, 'I think we should all make ourselves comfortable so that you can tell us all about this really simple idea. I'll get the biscuits, maybe Reginald can get the tea.'

While they were gone, Mom took my hand, her eyes watering as she did so.

'Kat,' she whispered. 'Please don't come up with anything that will put yourself in danger. I couldn't bear it if anything were to happen to you.'

'Mom, don't worry,' I reassured her. 'I won't be in danger at all. If everything goes according to plan, the only ones in danger will be Ailsa and her sisters. And, just out of curiosity, what exactly is the proper name for a collection of vampires?'

'Clan,' said Grandma, coming back into the room. 'There are lots of words such as *coven*, *pack*, and *brood*, but clan seems to be the most appropriate in this instance.'

'Clan, yes, that suits,' I agreed.

Pop came in with the tea, and everyone settled down ready for me to explain.

'Right,' I started. 'First problem is how to get the "clan" to return to the village. Well, the easy way is for me to be crowned Warrior Queen.'

That sentence sounded so much better in my head. Out loud it sounded like an attempt to be something that I wasn't entitled to be. 'I know I'm not the Queen,' I added, hastily, 'but if Ailsa thinks I am, that will be enough to attract them here, because they will want to dispose of the Queen before she can inherit her powers from Mother Earth.'

I could see Mom wasn't happy at all. In fact, I was sure she was just about to explode. But I carried on.

'Pop will be able to sense Ailsa getting close so, at that point we lure them into the basement of the farmhouse at Pets Corner and trap them there. I won't be in any danger because they won't get anywhere near me, Mom.'

Mom seemed to calm down a little. 'And how do you propose to do that?' she demanded.

'Well, and this is where we need permission from The Elders, I turn The Hooligoats into my Familiars, so they can take human form and lure the vampires into the basement. Once they are inside, The Hooligoats will turn back to being goats and run up the stairs, at which point we'll close up the doorway using iron sheeting.'

Pop look disappointed. 'And what would my part be?' he asked.

'We need you to be the early-warning system, Pop, to tell us when she's getting close. Also, you and Marcas and Mr Gohturd can get the basement rigged up with CCTV so that we can watch it all from here. But you three mustn't go anywhere near Ailsa and her chums, otherwise she'll be able to control you.'

'But, Kat,' sighed Mom. 'You won't be able to watch it all from the safety of the cottage at the same time as moving a heavy piece of iron across the doorway to the basement. That would take some serious strength.'

'How about the strength of a Canadian grizzly?' suggested Bronwen. 'That'd do it, for sure.'

After talking it through for a little while longer, Grandma was decided.

'Right, we're sorted. We have a Containment Team that can be here within a couple of hours. They'll be able to take the clan into custody. In fact, if we can take them alive, I know someone who'd love to meet them.'

'And turning The Hooligoats into Familiars?' I asked.

'We'll need to get The Elders involved to sanction the Coronation and to re-consider the restriction on the permitted number of Familiars, but that shouldn't be a problem. In fact, I think we should invite them here straight away to discuss it.'

Mom panicked. 'Here? But, but, how many of them are there?'

'There's ten, plus me, so eleven in all. Should fit into this room quite snugly.'

I was so excited that I jumped up and down. 'Yes, yes, go and phone them, Grandma, let's get this all sorted.'

Grandma paused for a while, keeping perfectly still, then she spoke again. 'Done. They can all come, they'll be here in a couple of hours' time.'

—

'Well, that was very odd,' I said to Marcas when we were sitting alone in the garden a little later. 'Up until now, Grandma has contacted the other Elders by telephone, then by going to see them in Dudley. Yet, just now, she seemed to communicate with them by thought transfer.'

'There's nothing about your grandma that surprises

me. I mean, I keep wondering how the Baobhan Sith knew about The Prophecy, while your mom didn't.'

'What makes you think the Baobhan Sith know about The Prophecy?'

'Well, your grandma says that Ailsa came here to the village in order to kill the Warrior Queen.'

'And?'

'So, how would they know about the Warrior Queen, without knowing about The Prophecy?'

'Er… Er… Er, that's a very good question.'

The two of us sat in silence. I was deep in thought, pondering over what Marcas had said. Once again, I couldn't help thinking that Grandma was holding stuff back from us. I just hoped that there wasn't anything that we actually needed to know. After all, and it only just sank in at that point in time, this wasn't a game any longer, there were lives at stake.

—

Half an hour later, Mom came rushing over to us.

'You two need to come through,' she urged. 'The Elders are here, and they're impatient to get started. Come on, quickly, and prepare for a surprise.'

Intrigued, Marcas and I went to the living room doorway and peered inside.

'Goodness,' muttered Marcas. 'Which one is your grandma? They all look very similar.'

'I don't think they're *similar*,' I replied. 'I think they're *identical*. They are all clones of Grandma. And all but one has a yellow Post-it note stuck to their forehead.'

Chapter Nineteen

And Twelve Makes?

———

'Kat and Marcas, about time too,' said the grandma without a Post-it note stuck to her head. 'Come in, have a seat and let me introduce you to everyone. Having said that, tee, hee, hee, hee, you'll probably be able to guess who they are. But in case you don't,' Grandma stood up and started to point to each of the others in turn, 'this is Grandma Two from Sedgley, and this is Grandma Eight, she's from Netherton. She's been watching over our young gerbil. This one, tee, hee, hee, hee, this is Grandma Four...'

'Stop, please,' I cried. 'I can see the numbers on the Post-it notes. I would like an explanation though, and which one of you is actually my grandma?'

'I am,' they all chorused, then burst into synchronised giggling.

'Oh dear,' I murmured. 'This is going to be a long meeting.'

'You're right, Kat,' said Grandma-without-a-Post-it-note. 'You deserve an explanation. So, I'm the one that's been here for the past few weeks. And, of course, I'm the one that actually gave birth to your mom, so I'm Grandma One. I invited all these other Grandmas and they've just arrived. They all live in, or around, Dudley. In fact, Grandma Seven over there by the fireplace hasn't been outside of Brierley Hill until today.'

'But why are you all the same? Why are you all Grandmas?'

'Well, remember I told you about Frankie Steiner and her experiments?'

'Oh, goodness, were you all made by Dr Steiner? How very confusing.'

'Not really, Kat,' said sitting-by-the-fireplace Grandma Seven. 'It makes for consistency of decision-making in The Elders.'

As one, they all nodded approvingly. 'Hmmm, Consistent Decision Making.'

'And,' continued Grandma Seven, 'if one of us loses the plot, the others can continue as though nothing had happened.'

This provoked a collective dismay. 'One of us lost the plot,' they all said resignedly.

'One of you lost the plot?'

'Well,' resumed Grandma One, 'there were originally twelve of us but we, kind of, lost one.'

'Lost one?'

'Indeed we did. Grandma Twelve was something of a wildcard, a bit rebellious.'

'I don't think she was religious at all,' complained by-the-ornamental-elephant Grandma, as she reached to turn up the volume on her hearing aid.

'Not religious, Grandma Six,' said Grandma One. 'Rebellious. REBELLIOUS!'

I was beginning to feel like one of the parrots at Pets Corner. 'Rebellious?' I repeated.

'Yes, she went off by herself. Formed a rather nasty cult somewhere in the Transylvania area.'

'Transylvania? That's where... Oh, dear, it didn't happen to be a vampire cult, did it?' I asked.

'Well guessed, and yes, it did. But that particular group were mostly males, and they were all a bit too wishy-washy for Grandma Twelve, so she left Transylvania and moved to the Highlands of Scotland. She formed another cult there, exclusively for females.'

I could see the pattern emerging. 'Was she the founding member of the Baobhan Sith, by any chance?'

'Er, yes she was. Though her Scottish accent is rubbish. It just sounds like somebody from Birmingham.'

'Noooo,' I exclaimed. 'Are you seriously telling me that we're about to go hunting for four of the most vicious monsters that the world has ever known, and one of them happens to be my grandma?'

'Well, it sounds bad when you say it like that,' admitted Grandma One. 'But, on the plus side, she *is* estranged...'

'She *is* estranged!' they all chorused, with more nodding of heads.

'Oh, dear.'

What else was there to be said?

The Coronation was a real disappointment. I was expecting that all of my Grandmas would organise a date and invite loads of Huldufólk to come along. Grandma One said there wasn't time for that so, there and then, they all gathered in a circle around me and chanted some old stuff that I didn't even understand, and put a party hat from an old Christmas cracker on my head. And that was it! Talk about ruining my big day.

Converting The Hooligoats was much more exciting, and funny. We walked them round to Sue Purman's garden, so that we'd have plenty of room, and we invited Mr Gohturd and Bronwen to come and watch. Turning a Familiar was supposed to be almost the same as shape-shifting myself, though the Grandmas had to do their bit first. I had to visualise the goats morphing into a human and, at the same time, the Grandmas chanted again, and took handfuls of rice confetti, which they sprinkled liberally over the lads. Ralph wasn't amused. He kept wittering about them using rice confetti when they could just as easily have used linseed chips. I don't think he was into symbolism.

To my amazement, as soon as they were finished, all of the Grandmas except Grandma One shook my hand and wished me luck, then announced they needed to get back home.

'They don't like to be away from Dudley for too long,' explained Grandma One, as the others all made their way out of the garden. 'They start having dizzy spells. No help at all when you're trying to catch vampires, I'm afraid. Not to worry, though, we've started using CynkMynd again, so we'll all know what's happening and, when the time is right, we'll open up to Grandma Twelve.'

'Sink what?' I asked.

'Basic telepathy between us Grandmas, courtesy of Frankie Steiner. Haven't needed it before, but I reckoned it might come in handy now, so we switched it on last time we were together.'

—

Grandma had warned me beforehand that it would take a few tries for me to get used to turning all four of them at the same time, so we decided it would be best if I tried just one of them to begin with, then work my way up. Once the ceremony was over, it was time to test my skills.

'Right,' I announced to the lads. 'I need a guinea pig.'

'Sorry,' bleated Fernando. 'There's only us goats here.'

'No, I don't mean an actual guinea pig, I mean I need one of you to experiment on.'

'Will it hurt? I'm not doing it if it hurts.'

Grandma bent down to scratch Fernando's ear. 'Would we do something that would hurt you?' she cooed sweetly.

'I have to have a booster injection every year. That hurts. Anyhow, turning us into human form was Ralph's idea. Why doesn't he go first?'

Grandma laughed. 'This won't hurt at all. In fact, when you're in human form, you'll be so tall you'll be able to reach the hayrack in Sue's shed without having to stand on your hind legs.'

That seemed to change Fernando's mind. 'Ooooh, really?' he quipped. 'In that case, I'll be first, please.'

As Fernando stood in front of me with an eager look on his face, I closed my eyes tight shut, and imagined him standing up straight and becoming human. When I opened them again a couple of minutes later, he'd gone.

'What happened?' I cried in horror. 'Have I killed him?'

Grandma laughed and pointed to the shed. 'He's in there.'

A face, mostly human and at about person-height, peered out at me. A strand of hay was sticking out of its mouth. The face spat the hay out.

Grandma could hardly speak for laughing. 'I only said you'd be able to reach it, tee, hee, hee, hee, not that you'd like it.'

I desperately wanted to see the results of my handywork. 'Fernando, come on out, let me look at you.'

It would be nice to say that Fernando walked out of the shed, but it was actually more of a stumble. I guess he found walking on two legs much more difficult than I had experienced when trying to walk on four. It was as though he'd put on some high-heeled shoes. But he persevered, bless him, and slowly made his way towards me. When he was standing in front of me, he made his first attempt at speaking.

''Ungry,' he muttered.

Back to the huh problem again, I thought.

'Hhhh, Hhhungry,' I corrected him.

'Well, if you're hhhh hhhungry as well, can we get some food?'

So my first attempt at modelling a pygmy goat as a human was not as bad as I thought it would be. The ears were an issue, but then I've never been any good with ears, as Ralph likes to point out. And the horns were still there. Otherwise, ten out of ten.

'I did tell you,' Grandma reminded me, 'that your ability to control the appearance of a Familiar would diminish once you added more. So, I suggest that you leave Fernando in human form, and try to turn one of the others.'

I closed my eyes again and concentrated hard on turning Cuthbert. This time, when I opened my eyes, Fernando and Cuthbert were both standing in front of me. Fernando's nose had slipped a little and, in addition to goat ears, horns and nose, Cuthbert's eyes didn't look quite right. Still, so far so good.

By the time I'd added Barney and Ralph, the four of them had very definite goat heads, but with human mouths. Ever so slightly bizarre, I know. Not the kind of thing you'd want to meet on a dark night, as Pop liked to say.

'Don't worry,' Grandma encouraged. 'When you first attempted to become a goat, it was the head that you didn't get right. I'm sure you can improve on this, over time.'

'But we don't have much time,' I said.

'Then you'd better get on with it.'

So I did.

The Hooligoats were all very patient with me, as I made attempt after attempt to turn all four of them into human form at the same time. Grandma helped a lot, especially when she reminded me that the goats wouldn't need to hold their human form for long. Just long enough, in fact, to attract the attention of the Baobhan Sith.

By the evening, I felt that I was beginning to get the hang of it. The goats had heads that resembled humans, all with the exception of the horns, which I couldn't get right no matter how hard I tried. All the work with Familiars did remind me of something, though.

'Grandma, where is your Familiar? I haven't seen her around for ages.'

'Gertie? Oh, she's fine. She reports back from time to time, but I sent her off on a special errand, so she'll probably be away for a while.'

When I asked about the errand, Grandma just went off to find some biscuits. *Typical Grandma*, I thought.

—

It didn't take Pop, Marcas and Mr Gohturd long to install CCTV cameras in the basement of the farmhouse. Marcas, despite his poorly leg, supplied the expertise. Obviously. Pop supplied the money. Obviously. It was all very hi-tech, as the cameras were cabled directly using ethernet something-or-other, they were infra-red something-else for seeing in the dark, and had hi-fi audio whatchamacallit (Marcas told me that. I have no idea what any of it means). The important thing is that there were two cameras in the basement and two that were spaced away from each other in the corridor that led to the basement. The cables ran next door to Sue Purman's house, and linked up to my laptop. Marcas tested connections, many times, and it all worked perfectly.

We also found some old, and very heavy, corrugated iron fencing sheets. One was heaved into place so that it blocked off the "secret" door to the basement, and Bronwen practised moving the other piece across the main basement door. The sheet was so heavy that she struggled at first to move it by herself, but she worked hard to develop her technique and, in the end, she could lever it over in just a matter of seconds.

With The Hooligoats well versed in what they had to do, everything was ready for a trial run.

Everyone, except Bronwen and The Hooligoats, gathered together in Sue's house and, at an agreed point, Pop spoke on the microphone to say that Ailsa was in range. Actually he didn't speak so much as shout. He's never got the hang of speaking quietly, even on a phone.

Once he'd done that, I turned The Hooligoats, who were already sitting in the basement, into human form and they repeated the words that I'd drummed into them. So far, so good. We waited a while, to simulate Ailsa and her clan going into the basement, then the Hooli-humans turned back to goats and legged it. As they raced through the door, Bronwen emerged from her hiding place in the downstairs loo, and slid the iron sheet into position. Perfect. We practised the whole thing another three times and, each time, we carefully monitored what was happening to try to spot any flaws in the process. But everything went as it was meant to do.

–

As we were all happy with the plan, it was time for Grandma to do her CynkMynd bit.

It wasn't long before she announced, 'The Elder Grandmas are ready to allow Grandma Twelve access. First thing in the morning, we'll open up the channel to her and she'll know that you've been crowned Warrior Queen.'

Grandma gave me an unexpected hug.

'You're worried,' she said gently, 'and you shouldn't be. Your plan is as good as it can be, and everyone knows what they have to do.'

'I know,' I said. 'But it's all going too well. I can't help feeling that I've missed something important. As though I'm being overly confident.'

'If you are missing something, then all of us have missed it. I certainly haven't spotted anything wrong, and we've practised as much as we can. Now, it's going to be a big day tomorrow. I've got the Containment Team on alert, so they're ready to come and get those creatures as soon as we have them secured. Time for sleep, I think.'

And so I went to bed. But I couldn't get the feeling out of my mind. That nagging feeling that there was something that I should be taking into account. Something really, really important.

Chapter Twenty
Best Laid Plans...

———

The weather on the following morning was beautiful. The sun shone in a clear blue sky. Birds sang. Although it wasn't my birthday until the following day, there were birthday presents waiting on the table for me.

'We know you're really anxious about today, so we thought they might cheer you up,' said Pop. 'Do you want to open one?'

'I can't open them yet,' I sighed. 'Tomorrow, when this is all over, then I'll open them.'

Pop, however, still insisted on leading everyone in the singing of 'Happy Birthday', not surprisingly using words that weren't in the original version. *Very rude*, I thought, though it did cheer me up.

And then we settled down to wait. Grandma had been certain that, once Grandma Twelve had picked up the CynkMynd connection with the other Grandmas, she would know that I had been crowned Queen. Suddenly, that actually seemed like a very dangerous thing to have suggested, but there was no way out of it now and I just had to trust that the plan would work without a hitch.

By ten o'clock, everyone started to get bored. Grandma hit the biscuits again. We watched the feed from the cameras to keep an eye on The Hooligoats, who were not used to being shut in a basement, and were starting to play-headbutt each other.

At about eleven o'clock, Pop suddenly clutched his head and cried out in pain. He stood, unable to move, his mouth trying to form words.

At last he shook his head, as though trying to clear it, and muttered, 'She's coming, I can sense her. Not far away.'

Grandma looked carefully at Pop. 'I wondered whether that might happen,' she said, then closed her eyes and chanted, slowly and quietly.

Pop flopped to the floor. We rushed to him.

'I'm okay,' he murmured. 'Do what you need to do. Quickly.'

I held Pop's hand as I closed my eyes and visualised The Hooligoats.

'They've changed, Kat, well done,' cried Mom, who was watching the camera feed intently.

'Now for the dangerous bit,' I said, as I spoke to the goats through the audio link.

The Hooli-humans put their hats on to hide their horns and started chatting with each other about how they were missing the friends that they knew when they were kids. Within seconds, the four Baobhan Sith were passing the cameras in the hallway of the farmhouse.

I couldn't resist asking, 'They all look the same. Which one is Grandma Twelve?'

'Couldn't tell you,' whispered Grandma. 'Long time has passed since I saw her last, and she's obviously changed her appearance since then. I sense her, though. She's here.'

I was beginning to feel more comfortable about things. So long as The Hooligoats did what they were supposed to do, things appeared to be going well.

As we watched the live feed from the cameras, the vampires appeared at the doorway into the basement, and we heard one of them speak.

'These humans smell so bad.'

'Such a disgusting odour,' said another.

'Men,' said the third. 'They never wash properly. They always stink. I have to hold my nose when I feed on them.'

'So long as they taste good,' said the fourth, 'what does the smell matter? Now, they have invited us in, so let's feed, we have been asleep for ages and I am ravenously hungry.'

They all slithered into the basement, and all watched in amazement as the Hooli-humans turned back to goat form and raced past them. The door shut behind them and we could see and hear Bronwen Bear sliding the iron plate into place.

We all erupted into cheering. We'd done it. The Baobhan Sith were trapped.

As our cheering subsided, we returned to look at the screen again.

'I don't remember them being able to do that, before,' said Grandma, as one of the vampires held her two hands together, palms inwards.

There was a light visible inside her hands, the intensity of it growing brighter and brighter until she opened her hands again, revealing a large ball of fire. She turned her hands outwards, and the fireball shot forward and smashed against the wooden door, which disintegrated in a curtain of flames. Once the smoke had cleared, we could see the iron plate behind it standing firm.

'Well, that was interesting,' said Grandma. 'I think we should get the Containment Team here sooner rather than later.'

Marcas changed the channel on the camera feed to the ones in the hallway. Bronwen Bear was lying motionless on the floor.

'What's happened to her?' shouted Mom.

'I don't know,' I replied. 'But I'm going over there to find out.'

I raced out and jumped over the low fence that separated the farmhouse from Sue's house. Mom was close behind me, followed by Grandma. The front door was wide open, and we could see Bronwen lying there in the hallway. Before we could get to her, though, there was a voice behind us.

'Hello, nice Huldufólk ladies. Good of you to come and see us. Though I don't think you were expecting us to get past your little trap, were you?'

The four vampires stood stock still outside the house, grinning widely at us.

In an instant, both Mom and Grandma shape-shifted, Grandma taking wing, and Mom running fast between the creatures. Mom almost made it, but one of the vampires struck out and caught her on the left flank as she ran past. Mom yelped, blood running freely from the top of her damaged leg. She carried on running, her left leg dragging behind her, until she crumpled in a heap a short distance away. She didn't move again. The vampires laughed.

'So,' one of them sneered, 'you're supposed to be the Warrior Queen, are you? And yet you do nothing.'

'That's because she is nothing. Nothing but a little Huldufólk girl,' screeched another.

'Maybe we should make her one of us. Then she would realise where the real power lies.'

'No. We don't need more of us,' a sickly smirk spread from one ear to the other. 'We only need her to die.'

Two of the creatures, still laughing, turned and started to levitate towards Mom. I tried to move towards her, but the other two blocked my way. There was nothing I could do.

I didn't see the creature swing her claws at me, I just felt a sharp, searing pain on my shoulder as I was flung into the air and landed heavily against the hedge. They came over to where I'd landed and stood leering over me. Blood was streaming from the wound in my arm.

'So, Warrior Queen, what are you going to do now? Do you think we don't know about The Prophecy?'

'The Prophecy?' I asked, trying to buy a little time so that I could think.

'Ha, it cannot save you, its words will do nothing for you. You cannot harness the power of Mother Earth. Not today.'

I didn't understand. 'Not today? Why not today?'

'You act as though you do not know, Warrior Queen, but The Prophecy says that you will only be able to gain your powers when you reach your twelfth birthday. And we just happen to know that the anniversary of your birth is tomorrow. So, you see, by the time tomorrow comes, you and the other Huldufólk will be long dead.'

She reached down towards me, then flailed her arms in the air as Grandma swooped in, a whole stream of bats flying in formation behind her.

'Brought the cavalry, Kat. Thought you might need some help,' she yawped as she flew past.

The bats flew up higher, ready to make another dive, but the first fireball from the vampires took out two of them. I couldn't make out which one was Grandma, but a constant volley of fire blasted through them all until there was not a single bat left in the sky. All of them lay, wings fluttering uselessly, on the scorched ground around me.

There was an anger growing within me, deep down. I felt there was something welling up, but nothing happened, only tears, which fell on the burnt grass. I cried. I'm not ashamed to say it. I cried, my whole body shaking as I sobbed.

All four of the vampires watched me, a look of contempt on their faces. The two standing over me were still smirking when a metal bar came flying through the air and pierced one through the heart, going straight through and striking the second one in exactly the same place. There was no blood. Each of them looked with horror at the other, then exploded in a blizzard of embers. The metal bar fell to the ground, and Pop was suddenly kneeling by my side.

'Javelin Champion, Tividale Comprehensive School,' he said, grinning. 'Now, let's get you out of here.'

Pop lifted me up, and started to carry me towards home, but we hadn't got very far before the other two creatures headed us off. One of them grabbed me and threw me back onto the ground, whilst the other one grabbed Pop by the neck, lifted him off the floor, and hurled him through the air. Pop lay still where he fell.

I managed to crawl on all fours to Pop. I had the feeling the two remaining vampires were just playing with me the way a cat would play with a wounded mouse.

'I'm okay,' Pop winced. 'Just winded. I'll be back on my feet when I can catch my breath.'

Just then, Mom called out for help. The vampire nearest to me hesitated, then started to move away.

'This one can wait, let us deal with the wolf lady once and for all.'

I struggled to my knees, not knowing what to do.

There was a gentle voice behind me. 'Hello, Kat, can I be of any assistance?'

I eased my body round to see who it was. Mrs Bradbury was standing there.

'Mrs Bradbury, I never thought I'd be so glad to see you,' I said, gratefully. 'If you can help Pop, I'll try to get over to Mom before those monsters get her.'

'Of course, dear,' she said sweetly.

I got to my feet and lunged forward as best I could towards where Mom lay. The vampires were almost on her, but they suddenly stopped and turned to watch what was happening behind me.

And then it occurred to me. The bit of the jigsaw that I was missing. I stopped still in my tracks, a feeling of dread washing over me. Mrs Bradbury had disappeared when Ailsa had gone, and just a small amount of her blood had been found. She hadn't been killed by Ailsa, she'd been turned. Mrs Bradbury had become one of them, a Baobhan Sith, a vampire. She must have been the one who attacked Bronwen and let the others out of the basement.

I turned and looked back to where Pop was lying on the ground. Mrs Bradbury was over him, sucking in a green vapour from his mouth. She was taking his lifeforce. She was killing him.

I screamed long and loud. As I started to hobble painfully back towards Pop, there was a blur to my side as The Hooligoats, unexpectedly with Fernando in the lead, charged past with heads down. Fernando was only small, but he rammed Mrs Bradbury hard in the backside and she rolled over and over on the ground.

'That's for setting Bogrott on us, you monster,' muttered Fernando as he gasped for breath.

The others piled in, doing their best to stop her from getting to her feet and, for a short while, they succeeded. She rolled towards her pitchfork, which was propped up against the fence, and lunged at the lads with it, forcing them to retreat to a safe distance. They'd bought time, however, for me to grab the bar that Pop had used as a javelin, and I held it in front of me as Mrs Bradbury sped towards me with the pitchfork. The two prongs of the fork went either side of me, but my bar rammed home, straight through her heart. There was another shower of sparks, and Mrs Bradbury was no more.

–

While the remaining two Baobhan Sith looked on with sickly grins on their faces, I lifted Pop's head gently. I knew I was too late. I knew he was dead.

I cradled his lifeless body in my arms, letting my tears fall onto his face. There was no describing my feelings; I was empty, and lost. My best ever friend was dead. And I was the one who'd left him alone with his killer.

I saw Mom, as she struggled to crawl over to us, leaving a trail of blood as she went. She looked at Pop, and she too wept. The vampires were enjoying the whole spectacle.

'He's gone, Kat,' she sobbed.

'No, he can't be. Not Pop,' I said. 'Our magic, surely we must be able to bring him back.'

'No, Kat.' Mom laid her hand on mine. 'Not even our magic is strong enough to overcome death.'

–

The day had started out so hopeful, so easy, and I couldn't believe this was how it was going to end. I looked around me at the devastation, and I wished and wished with all my heart that I could change it all. I took one deep breath after another, the loss of Pop tearing through me, the pain intensifying until I felt I would burst.

As my tears continued to fall, it dawned on me

that my loss, my pain, was an echo of something much bigger, something that Mother Earth must have been experiencing for a long time. Her rainforests decimated, her oceans overwhelmed with plastic waste, her lands torn apart by mining, by fracking, her atmosphere polluted. She was in so much pain. No wonder Grandma had said that she could feel her trembling.

I don't know what good I thought it would do. I guess I just felt that I was sharing a common hurt with Mother Earth. As exhaustion began to overwhelm me, I knelt down and gently kissed the scarred and blackened soil. Thoughts raced round my head like a whirlwind and, in my tiredness, I started talking to myself.

'I felt I could do this. And now I've failed,' I muttered.

Words formed inside my mind. *The battle isn't over. It's only just beginning.*

I nodded. 'That's right. I've lost Pop, Grandma as well, but I'm not scared of these creatures. I have to save Mom.'

The words inside my head became louder. *Young elf, your courage has never been in doubt. All you need is a little help.*

As I raised my head and readied myself to stand, The Hooligoats gathered in front of me.

'Kat,' said Fernando in a hushed voice. 'Can you feel that?'

The ground began to tremble beneath me. With my heart beating faster, I reached down and placed my hand flat against the blackened soil. Where it was scorched, tiny shoots of grass began to sprout again, growing taller and thicker with each tear that fell upon it. And I could feel something quite strange. Where my hands touched the fledgling grass, sparks began to crackle around them, then arc from the ground to my hand. It started as a trickle, but quickly grew until streams of sparks covered me from head to toe, and I felt as though I could sense everything in the world. It was then that I knew that Mother Earth was with me, giving me strength, giving me power. The exhaustion of a few moments ago evaporated, and I stood up straight and levelled my gaze at the two vampires. I watched their mocking sneers turn to terror as huge, orange-red wings unfurled from my sides.

I grew larger, towering over them as I gained in height, my legs grew and bent, and I could feel my muscles tensing as they strengthened. I looked down, not at my shoes, not at my dainty little hooves, but at the legs and body of a lioness. Sleek, powerful, with a red sheen that screamed out its warning of danger. I crouched low to the ground and then, lifting my head high, I thrust upward and let out a roar that resonated around the village.

I rose up into the air, effortlessly gaining height as my wings beat steadily. Then I heard a flapping and a voice beside my ear.

'About time too, my Warrior Queen.'

'Grandma! I thought you were…'

'Dead? Nope, just a bit of mental projection. I was giving you time to get yourself sorted. Now, I think we need to deal with those two miscreants, don't you?'

With Grandma at my wingtip, I flew upwards until the world below me seemed to be in miniature, then swooped down at the two creatures who, by now, were desperately trying to escape across the surrounding fields with Fernando and the other Hooligoats in hot pursuit. As I soared downwards, they stopped and shot out fireball after fireball, all of which just glanced harmlessly off me. Finally, they shielded their heads with their arms, but there was no point. When I was within reach, a single blow from my claws was enough. The vampires exploded into nothingness.

–

Grandma and I landed close to where Pop's body lay, and both of us resumed human form. Mom was still clinging on to Pop's hand. The Hooligoats rushed back to stand by her. Even Barney had tears running down his cheeks.

'Grandma, Mom says our magic is not powerful enough, but I can't lose Pop. I am the Warrior Queen now, surely that means something. If my power can't bring him back, what is the point of it? Show me how to save him, bring him back to me.'

Grandma shook her head. 'Your strength, your power, your magic will be needed in an ongoing battle against all of the nightmares that are about to unleash their horrors on this world. But it's not strong enough to overcome the death of a human, no matter how much you loved him.'

'But The Prophecy was wrong. One of the vampires said that I couldn't inherit these powers until the day of my twelfth birthday. So maybe you don't know everything about my powers.'

Grandma laid her hand gently on my arm and spoke softly. 'When Dr Steiner made the Grandmas, we knew from The Prophesy that one of them would be unstable. After some discreet testing, it was obvious that Grandma Twelve was the weak link. We gave her an altered Prophesy so that she wouldn't know that you could inherit your powers on the last full day of your twelfth year. All you need to know now, Kat, my Queen, is that almost every single thing that has happened was predicted. The one and only thing we couldn't be sure of was whether you would be able to connect with Mother Earth. If you hadn't, evil would have prevailed.'

'You knew?' I said incredulously. 'Everything? And Pop's death? Did you know about that? Was that prophesied?'

Grandma nodded. 'Pop is gone and, as Huldufólk, we cannot change that. But he fought as a hero, and we should honour him as such. His body will be preserved in a casket of ice, so that Huldufólk may come from all around to pay their respects.'

I could only stare at Grandma. I had no words.

'Now,' said Grandma quietly. 'I will set up the casket for Pop, but then I must go. Gertie has succeeded in her mission and I have to go to her. Mr Gohturd is looking after Bronwen, and you must take care of your mother.'

'And Marcas?' I asked. 'Where is Marcas?'

Grandma shook her head. 'Haven't seen him around for a while. I'm sure he'll surface soon.'

Grandma lifted Pop's body as though it was weightless, and carried him over to Sue's garden, to a part of it sheltered by a large apple tree. As she waved her hands over his corpse, ice formed around him, completely enclosing him.

There was a flutter of wings. Grandma was gone, and Mom, The Hooligoats, and I were left alone with the frozen casket that now held Pop.

Chapter Twenty-One
And Suet Begins...

———

So, there you go.

Whenever I used to say that, Pop would just respond by saying, 'Well, where *do* I go, Kat?' I can't help but hiccup a laugh to myself.

Still, you're right up to date now, and you know as much as me. It's my birthday today and, as I said at the beginning, it's not a day for celebration, not with Pop gone. I just so wish I'd opened the birthday presents yesterday, when he was still around. I did manage to open one of them this morning: It was the most beautiful hat I've ever seen. A soft, green, felt one with a wide brim and a floppy, pointy top. And there was a note from Pop that said, 'To my very special elf.' It made me cry, so I didn't open any more.

I can hardly believe he's gone. I know I still talk about him as though he were alive, as though he might walk through the front door and tell me he's been for a 'yomp around the Big, Wide World'. He won't, of course, he's still in the casket of ice that was made for him by Grandma's magic and, already, some Huldufólk have started coming along to see him, to pay their respects to their human hero. And I have to be strong now, ready to face up to whatever comes next.

Unfortunately, of course, Grandma missed all of this. She went off without saying goodbye, right after freezing Pop. She didn't show it, but I think she was as upset as Mom and I were. After all, she knew The Prophecy, she knew Pop was going to die.

But I do have Marcas' friendship. We held hands for a long time last night, just trying to come to terms with everything. Sleep was impossible for any of us, of course, including The Hooligoats, who played such a brave and amazing part in what happened yesterday. They've already insisted they want to be part of the team for the next monster-hunt. And, yes, you're right, we should change Fernie's nickname. From now on he'll be known as *Fernando the Fearless*.

Mom, Bronwen and Mr Gohturd are resting in the kitchen at the moment. I don't think Mom knows quite what to do. She certainly has never drunk so much tea. Bronwen has helped to heal her wounds, though, so she'll be okay. Eventually.

Of course, I'm telling you all this so that others are aware of what's happening around us. The Baobhan Sith were just the first. There will be more, and we all need to prepare. Here in the village, we had such violent lightning strikes this morning, and I have no idea yet what caused that. It may be that another threat is already here.

What we do know for certain, though, having found

one of the maps in Grandma's suitcase, is that the ice fortress that was keeping Krampus imprisoned has been found empty. Krampus used to be a companion of Father Christmas, so I'm told, and gained the nickname Santa Claws because he wasn't quite as nice to children as Saint Nick. In fact, he was incarcerated because he had a habit of finding the children on the Naughty List, and eating them. Bit drastic, but there you go. Again.

Odd, isn't it, when you think about it? So many people don't believe in Santa Claus, but I'm actually about to start hunting his sidekick before he finds the first Naughty List. Global Warming has a lot to answer for you know.

Hang on, I hear the doorbell. Let me just see who it is and then I'll be back with you.

—

'Oh, hello Mr Bogrott, I wasn't expecting you to turn up.'

'Goodly morrowning, jung miss. I juss fort I'd come an say, on beharf o' me missus an me, 'ow sorry we am 'bout yer dad.'

'That's very kind of you, Mr Bogrott. Thank you.'

'Anywaysup, Agnes as bin cookin, an she's med this fer yow.'

'Er, what is it?'

'A Suet Puddin' iswotitis, med to a repicee wot is undrids o'yeyers owd.'

'That, er sounds nice. It doesn't have meat in it, does it?'

'Corse it duz. Theyers arf a cow in theyer. Guz luvly wiv orange chips.'

- 197 -

'Ah, well. Erm, thank you all the same, it really is very kind of you to think of us, but we're all vegetarians here.'

'Wot's one o'them, then?'

'Vegetarian? For us, it means we don't eat meat, or anything with meat in it.'

'Wot? Nun at all? Yow muss be coddin us.'

'No, I'm not joking with you, we really don't eat meat.'

'Okay, tell yer wot, then. How baht the missus duz one wiv juss chickin in it?'

'That's still meat, Mr Bogrott. So, erm…'

'Is it? I s'pose it muss be. Ah, well, how baht this then, how baht a scrummy gooosbry pie?'

'Fruit. Yes, that would be perfect, thank you.'

'Theyer yer goo, then. Gooosbry pie it is. I'll be back in two sherkes of a lamb's tayal. See yer in a bit.'

—

Sorry about the interruption. I've asked Mom to see to any more callers, so we should be undisturbed now. So where was I? Oh, yes, I was telling you about Krampus. It seems The Elders have drawn up a plan to… Sorry, that's the doorbell again. Mr Bogrott must have raced to get the gooseberry pie back here so quickly. We should be okay, though, Mom will answer it. As I was saying, The Elders have… Oh dear, Mom sounds as though she's getting hysterical, sorry for yet another interruption, but I'd better go and che—

'Oh, Grandma, Gertie, you're both back. Come on in, I was just talking about what's happened over the past few weeks.'

'My Queen, it's good to see you again.'

'Not Queen, please Grandma. Kat will do. Maybe even The Kat? And who is this lady with you?'

'I am Dr Francine Nevaeh Steiner. Frankie N Steiner to my friends. It's an honour to be of service to… Queen The Kat.'

'To be of service? I don't understand. And why are you all grinning like that?'

'Your grandma and I, we have been working on… ah, but maybe best for Queen The Kat to come and see for self. Yes?'

'AHOOOOOOOOOOOL!'

—

And Suet Continues…

In

The Kat and The Hooligoats – The Curs of The Weirdwolf

Don't miss the next instalment in the adventures of Kat and the four pygmy goats, when the past comes back to haunt them in unexpected, and unpleasant, ways…

**Check in to – barryhudleyauthor.co.uk
for updates and information.**

 Matador

For exclusive discounts on Matador titles,
sign up to our occasional newsletter at
troubador.co.uk/bookshop